The ceremony was about to begin

One thing that Frances found troubling was a neckline cut low enough to make her feel brazen. She frowned. "Sabelita, I can't possibly wear this dress, it makes me feel too...too...."

"Seductive?" Sabelita suggested slyly, casting a look of approval at curves bulging over the top of her dress.

Frances swung round just in time to see Sabelita hurrying out to make way for a strange Gypsy male.

"Would you kindly not walk into my tent unannounced," she began, then took a step backward. The flashing-eyed man wearing tight breeches tucked into the tops of knee-length leather boots and a silken shirt with wide sleeves gathered at the wrist, was the aloof, rarely smiling Conde.

But whereas she was startled, he appeared stunned as silently he eyed her appearance. *"Madre de Dios!"* he murmured with an audacity that was pure Romany. "Have I the courage to flaunt such temptation before a tribe of macho Gypsy males?"

Lord of
the Land

Margaret Rome

Harlequin Books

TORONTO • NEW YORK • LOS ANGELES • LONDON
AMSTERDAM • PARIS • SYDNEY • HAMBURG
STOCKHOLM • ATHENS • TOKYO • MILAN

Original hardcover edition published in 1983
by Mills & Boon Limited

ISBN 0-373-02561-0

Harlequin Romance first edition July 1983

CHAPTER ONE

IT was dusk by the time the taxi Frances had hired to transport her from the airport finally swept inside a cobbled courtyard and drew up in front of a simple yet impressive white building fronted by a massive old oak door.

'El Palacio de Rocio, *señorita*!' With an indolent wave the driver indicated the building once used as a hunting lodge by Spanish aristocracy but which was now the headquarters of scientists attached to a nature reserve made up of miles of undisturbed heathland and stone-pine woods that attracted innumerable bird species pausing to rest and feed during their migrations to and from Africa, sometimes lingering all winter and remaining to breed.

'Thank you—*gracias* . . .!' she amended, scrambling hastily from the back seat when the gum-chewing driver made no move to assist her to alight. He had emphasised his resentment at being forced into absenting himself from frequent and consequently more lucrative fares by stowing her one large suitcase at her feet instead of placing it inside the boot, and as she began struggling to manoeuvre its awkward bulk over the sill the sound of a savage imprecation directed at the driver shot her bent spine erect.

'*Languido paseante, muévate l De prisa! Pronto!*'
When Frances's startled head jerked upright to

5

connect with an audible crack against the roof of the taxi a further spate of Spanish invective, too rapid for her to follow, erupted from the man who began hurrying down the steps towards her.

Belatedly, the galvanised driver heaved out of his seat to assist her, then drew back when his arrival at her side coincided exactly with that of the contemptuous man who, according to the little she was able to gather, knew the driver's family history well enough to condemn him as a worthy successor of generations of ignorant, unchivalrous, idle dogs.

'Please don't upset yourself on my behalf, *señor*,' she interceded weakly, stunned as much by the verbal onslaught as by the crack upon her head, 'there's really no need, I'm quite used to managing for myself.'

The irate Spaniard spun on his heel, his frown replaced by a look of astonishment.

'You are English!' he seemed almost to accuse. Then once again his features darkened. 'A thousand apologies, *señorita*—to have had to witness uncavalier treatment being meted out to one of your sex is bad enough, but the fact that you are a visitor to our country makes this man's behaviour even more indefensible. May I ask why you are travelling so far off the beaten track—are you on your way to visit friends, or even lost, perhaps?'

'Neither,' she assured him in a breathless rush. 'I have a room reserved here at the Palacio de Rocio.' Nervously, she began fumbling in her handbag. 'My name is Frances Ross.'

When the Spaniard's look of concern vanished, leaving him tight-mouthed, eyes narrowed with suspicion, she felt an instant affinity with the subdued taxi driver.

'Perhaps I had better introduce myself, *señorita*,' he suggested frostily. 'I am Dr Bernado Ribera, director of the Rocio Nature Reserve. As you so correctly stated, a room has been reserved for Dr Francis Ross, the eminent ornithologist, author of several books which his many admirers, including myself, claim to be the most detailed and comprehensive of any dealing with that particular subject. Inside the dust cover of each book is a photograph of the author, showing him to be bearded, rather elderly, and very definitely *male*.'

For the past couple of months Frances had been called upon to exercise great control over stricken emotions in order to present a brave face to friends whose pressing invitations to dine or attend numerous social gatherings had only succeeded in emphasising her loss, nevertheless, the brief word-portrait of her father caused her a wince, rendered clear grey eyes dark with pain.

'I'm Frances with an "e",' she responded simply, 'the late Dr Ross's daughter.'

'The late . . .!' Dr Ribera hesitated, obviously stunned, and because fatigue had rendered her incapable of listening to further expressions of condolence without collapsing into tears she rushed into a choked explanation.

'My father's death was very sudden . . . a fatal heart attack, totally unexpected . . . so far as I'm aware he hadn't suffered a day's illness in his entire life. I know that you and he often exchanged correspondence, Doctor, because it was I who typed his letters, his manuscripts, corrected the proofs of his books and made all his travelling arrangements. He was so looking forward to visiting the Rocio Reserve, to meeting you in person, and he was especially excited by the prospect of being given an opportunity to study the habits of one of the rarest birds in Europe whose chief nesting ground is in the region of the Reserve—the Spanish imperial eagle.'

She blinked hard, hoping his compassionate eyes would remain blind to the glint of tears, that his nature would be sensitive enough to perceive that what she was most in need of was rest and the solitude of a private room. Desperate to stave off a threatened breakdown, she groped inside her handbag for the required number of notes and extended her fare towards the shifting, obviously uncomfortable driver.

'*Gracias*, I think you will find that the amount is correct.'

'*Un momento!*' As if anxious to perform any service that might help to communicate his wealth of pity for the slender, drooping girl who had landed on his doorstep, Dr Ribera snatched the notes out of reach of the driver, checked their value, then casting him a look of scorn, calmly divided the wad and thrust a substantial number back into her handbag.

'*Marcharse!*' he dismissed, handing the depleted wad to the scowling driver. Then turning his back he directed his complete attention towards her.

'Welcome to the Palacio de Rocio, *señorita*,' he smiled, cupping a hand beneath her elbow to urge her gently up the steps leading towards the immense oak door. 'There is still much to be discussed, but for the moment explanations can wait, our first priority must be to ensure that you are given adequate time to rest.'

She was capable of no more than a smile of gratitude, but seemingly it was enough, for after escorting her across a width of hallway and summoning a maid to show her to her room he delayed her ascent of a highly polished staircase just long enough to inform her:

'We Spaniards are not in the habit of dining early, *señorita*, but this evening, in order to accommodate a very special guest whose arrival will be delayed because of a previous engagement, we shall be dining even later than usual. Because he regards your father's work so highly, this gentleman insisted upon rearranging his schedule in order to extend a personal welcome on the first day of your father's expected arrival in Andalusia. Unfortunately,' he shrugged, 'as he has always insisted upon remaining beyond the bounds of easy communication, it will be impossible to send a message informing him of the change of circumstances. I'm certain, however,' his dark brown eyes cast a hopeful look of appeal, 'that your presence at the dinner table would help to ease our guest's disappointment. I know that you must be extremely tired, *señorita*, but dinner will not be served until at least ten o'clock, so if after a short rest you feel tempted to join us, I'm certain you would find El Conde most appreciative.'

With one hand upon the balustrade supporting aching limbs urging her to refuse, Frances hesitated. An aeon seemed to have passed since she had left home shortly after dawn that morning, hours filled with travelling by coach and by train, of hanging around airports in England and in Spain, of flying—which she detested only slightly less than the noise, crowds and inevitable fatigue that had accompanied every mile of her journey. Yet Dr Ribera had shown her such kindness, had forborne to ask questions even though there were gaps in his knowledge he must be aching to have filled. Also, El Conde, whoever he might be, deserved consideration, if only because of his stated admiration of her father's work.

'I should be honoured to join you for dinner, Doctor,' she accepted with a wan smile, her eyes set like pools of grey mist in a pale, pointed face. 'If you could arrange it, I'd like someone to waken me with a call around nine o'clock.'

The maid closed the shutters and drew curtains across the window immediately they entered a cool, spacious bedroom, then she opened a door to indicate with a flourish a well appointed bathroom with walls of sparkling tiles, a mirror, vanity basin, and a stack of thick white towels.

But Frances had eyes for only the narrow single bed made up with crisply laundered sheets, plump pillows, and a striped, drawn-back counterpane.

'*Muchas gracias*,' she nodded, battling to suppress a yawn, then immediately the door had closed behind the smiling maid she kicked off her shoes and stretched out upon the bed, meaning to snatch five minutes of complete relaxation before attempting the tiresome chore of undressing.

But as so often happens when endurance has

been stretched to the peak of fatigue, the moment her body relaxed her mind began racing over the events of the day, the purpose of her visit to Andalusia, and the traumatic loss that had led her towards the conviction that to take over where her father had left off was not merely a necessity but a bounden duty.

She and her father had been so close. Her pride in the world-wide acclaim his work had received had been more than sufficient reward for the many hours of hard work she had put in behind the scenes, organising and planning his many excursions to remote corners of the globe in search of rare and almost extinct species of wildlife that had been driven there to escape the pollution that inevitably follows man's ceaseless encroachment upon normal breeding grounds.

In common with many scholastic men, her father had possessed no aptitude for the mechanics of modern-day life—even the opening of a tin had been beyond him—so when the departure of the last of a long line of housekeepers had coincided with her own graduation from teachers' training college, she had sacrificed her ambitions without a qualm when he had pleaded:

'I have neither the patience nor the time to spare for interviewing prospective housekeepers. Also, I am appalled at the prospect of having to introduce yet another strange female into my household. I'm certain you could cope, Frances—with a daily helper, of course—you're such a capable child,' he had sighed. 'Whenever you come home the house is immediately filled with an atmosphere of calm serenity. I need you with me, and after all, there'd

be no great sacrifice involved in forgoing a career
that you haven't yet embarked upon.'

Somehow, she had stifled the protest that her
love of teaching was secondary only to her love of
children, and also that being confined for
innumerable hours each day within a house visited
only by his male contemporaries would result in
her losing touch with friends of her own age. But
she had schooled herself to accept that because of
the importance of his work her father's needs had
to be given first priority.

During the following two years, as her role of
housekeeper had been stretched to encompass the
duties of secretary, researcher, confidante, and
even co-author of his last book, she had suffered
only one regret—that fate should have deprived
him of a lifelong ambition to study at first hand
the habits of one of the world's rarest birds, the
bird that had been responsible for delaying
completion of his manuscript because he had
planned to devote to it the entire final chapter.

She drifted into sleep with her father's murmured
description running through her mind.

*'The Spanish imperial eagle is an arrogant loner,
possessing poise bestowed only upon those in
positions of power. A magnificent despot, whose
domain must be approached with caution, a proud
rebel who refuses to follow the example of the rest
of his species who nest in inaccessible mountains,
but provides proof of his courage by lording over the
plains, building his huge, sprawling nest in low
stone-pines as if deliberately challenging would-be
raiders of rare eggs who search the skies for
evidence of his presence, confidently assured of*

identifying him in flight because of striking snow-white markings on the leading edge of his wings that render him doubly vulnerable.'

'*Señorita*! It is nine o'clock, time to get up!'

A hesitant, heavily accented voice intruded into a dream filled with the sound of beating wings.

'Go away . . . go away . . .' Frances murmured restlessly, tossing her arms above her head to flail the air. Then suddenly she shot upright, wide awake and relieved to discover that she was alone in her room and that no fierce beaked predator was hovering overhead.

'Oh, *gracias* . . .' she stammered, then sank back against her pillows, confused by the beating noise still reverberating in her ears.

But when she stumbled across the room to throw back the shutters in search of air, realisation dawned at the sight of a helicopter, its landing lights flashing, lowering towards a stretch of flat ground to the rear of the Palacio. The noise that had accompanied her from sleep into wakefulness had been no more than the whirling of rotor blades causing a draught strong enough to whip branches of garden trees into a frenzy.

Guessing that she was witnessing the arrival of El Conde, Frances fled towards the bathroom where after a quick shower she began rooting through a suitcase crammed with denim jeans and cotton tops in search of the one dress she had included more or less as an afterthought.

It was white, simply cut and unadorned as a nun's habit. Hopelessly, she eyed her reflection in a mirror, conscious that it was crying out for the accessories she invariably wore with it—a necklace of brilliant blue beads with matching earrings that had been a gift from her father, bought in some native bazaar and presented with the comment:

'I thought of you immediately I spotted these, Frances dear. Blue is a colour that you should wear often, it adds violet depths to grey eyes and contrasts superbly against hair pale as silver. If only I could afford to buy you sapphires,' he had sighed, 'but at least the cornelian is your birth stone and the gem is purported to bestow contentment upon its owner—a blessing for which many would gladly exchange wealth!'

Blinking back tears of sadness, Frances moved away from the mirror, depressed by the knowledge that she could do nothing more to improve her appearance, that she was exactly what her image projected—simple, unassuming Frances, a dabbler in this and that but expert at nothing; a filler-in of backgrounds against which brilliance shone more brightly; a pair of willing hands; feet that were continuously on the move running errands for others; a nature too easily wounded by an unkind word; a small, pointed face; pale skin and a head that was too often bowed, waiting like the delicate snowdrop for some caring finger to tilt its petals towards the sun.

Upset by her thoughts, greatly missing the confidence she drew from her sparkling blue beads, she responded without enthusiasm to a rap upon the door and suffered a wave of panic when, after opening it, she saw Dr Ribero waiting on the threshold obviously agog.

'El Conde has arrived and is waiting to meet you, *señorita*!' His note of pride and air of suppressed excitement seemed to indicate that she was about to be greatly honoured. 'If you are quite ready,' he proffered an obliging arm, 'I will escort you to him immediately.'

Never had a passageway seemed so long, a staircase so extended, a *salón*, when they eventually entered it, so steeped with one man's presence. Every item of furniture, polished to perfection in preparation for his visit, seemed to be standing to stiff attention. Crystal vases glistened, silver glowed, cushions billowed proudly beneath un-creased velvet covers, yet the personage awaiting their arrival appeared quite unimpressed, patronis-ing as a rich grandee visiting the home of a peasant. All this Frances sensed in the first split second, but the impression remained, even strengthened, when he advanced to chill her to the bone with one terse, clipped sentence.

'Roberto tells me that you arrived here with the intention of travelling alone into the interior. This cannot be permitted, of course. Tomorrow I will accompany you to the airport and arrange your departure to England on the first available flight.'

Her gasped response was a mixture of outrage and startled wonder. She stared wide-eyed, her mouth rounded as a child's confronted by the unknown, a species of intimidating, domineering male whose profile looked chiselled from teak, whose eyes glinted ice-hard over dark, mysterious depths, whose hair winged blue-black except at the temples where white streaks stood out, shocking as a mark of Cain—an identifying trait that recalled immediately to her mind the words her father had used to describe the Spanish imperial eagle:

'*striking snow-white markings on the leading edge of his wings that render him doubly vulnerable.*'

But there appeared to be nothing in the least vulnerable about the man who had just taken imperious control over her affairs.

As if alert to signs of rebellion in the tightening of her lips, in the sudden bunching of fists behind her back, Dr Ribera attempted a conciliatory move by intervening swiftly:

'How remiss of me not to have effected a proper introduction—please allow me to rectify the omission immediately!' He stepped nearer, eyeing them nervously as a mediator caught between a pair of antagonists.

'Conde, you are already aware that Señorita Frances Ross is the daughter of the late Dr Ross whose work you so greatly admire. *Señorita,*' he turned towards her with a flourish, 'I am honoured to present to you El Conde Romanes del Nomadas y Aquila!'

Too annoyed to pretend pleasure, Frances nodded briefly, then proved herself totally un-impressed by launching her delayed attack.

'Obviously, Conde, you are accustomed to having your orders carried out with blind obedience, whereas I am a member of a notably stubborn race, amenable only to reason. However, if you should care to offer an explanation for your extraordinary directive, I promise to give it serious consideration?'

When a blade-straight nose flared at the nostrils she experienced an inner quivering, but stood her ground, hiding her apprehension behind a mask of serenity.

'I never waste time with words of explanation,' he froze her with a look, 'friends do not expect them and enemies merely use them as an excuse for argument.'

'But as I fall into neither category,' she insisted calmly, 'I feel I'm entitled to be given a reason for my dismissal.'

'The fact that the reasoning behind my decision is not clearly self-evident indicates a great lack of propriety in your upbringing, *señorita*. However, I once heard mentioned the fact that your father became a widower just a short time after his marriage and that he reared you, his only child, unaided, therefore perhaps we should not judge him too harshly. Here in Andalusia, females are cossetted from the cradle to the grave, protected as rare, fragile flowers firstly by fathers and brothers and then later by husbands and sons. This chivalrous attitude towards the opposite sex is not merely instilled from birth but has for centuries been ingrained into the characters of the men of Andalusia, which is why I—and Dr Ribera also—feel it our duty to ensure that you are protected from your own foolishness. Our womenfolk do not travel unescorted from house to house, much less through the marshes of a river delta where the utter loneliness and desolation has to be experienced to be believed. Why, *señorita*, do you suppose that thousands of birds regularly choose this region as a resting place during their seasonal migrations? It is because the marshes are a wilderness, one of the few remaining areas of immense solitude where birds can rest, feed, and breed without fear of human intrusion.'

She stared, speechless with resentment. In spite of having been warned that Andalusia was the Spain that had remained faithful to the reign of the Moor, a region where Carmens flirted behind fan and mantilla; where men dressed and acted like chivalrous Don Juans; where bullfights and gypsy flamenco were still favourite pastimes, it still seemed to her incredible that such outmoded customs could exist in a province just a stone throw away from the sophisticated Costa del Sol, where females sunbathed almost nude on beaches packed with oiled bodies grilling in the sun. Dimly, she began to suspect that there might be some truth in the legend that told of a knight errant tilting at windmills. El Conde Romanes del Nomadas y Aquila was comparatively young, yet his behaviour was that of a man belonging to an earlier age, an age when boys were trained in polite behaviour and grew up to be thorough gentlemen, always courteous towards women, self-possessed in the company of men, respectful and dutiful towards parents. Yet obviously, behind his façade of polite *fidalgo*, there lured the presence of Berberish unrest—a conflict of proud and passionate blood—a ruthless streak inherited perhaps from the God of Islam commonly represented as a pitiless tyrant who plays with humanity as on a chessboard and works out his game without regard to the sacrifice of the pieces.

Tentatively, she cleared her throat, feeling scared half out of her wits, yet determined not to be browbeaten.

'I'm sorry to have to admit, Conde, that I find

your remarks unconvincing, even downright contradictory. You must surely be aware that most girls of my generation would regard the treatment meted out to Andalusian women as little short of purdah? For many years now the battle for equality of the sexes has raged, and though we cannot yet claim to have achieved every one of our aims, women have at least managed to gain recognition as individuals. No longer can we lawfully be regarded or treated as mere male appendages, *señor*. We are free of the bonds imposed upon us by tradition, free to follow our own inclinations without interference from biased males. It is my wish to finish my father's last manuscript, and in order to do so I must be allowed access to the breeding grounds of the Spanish imperial eagle. If all Andalusian men are as chivalrous as you claim then what need have I of a chaperone?' she challenged with the triumph of one holding the last trump card. 'Even a man as resistant as yourself to change must eventually admit the futility of expecting one lordly Andalusian finger to plug a hole in the dam of progress!'

'*Progress*!' She jumped back a yard when the explosive word coincided with a fist thumping hard into El Conde's palm. 'Only fools are open to the conviction that to take a step forward is *always* a good idea! For every hundred steps man advances, our wildlife retreats one hundred and one! You came to Andalusia to study the habits of an extremely rare bird, did you not, *señorita*? Tell me, did you never stop to consider that, if men of vision had not resisted the advance of the progress you so vehemently support, you would not now be in any position to even anticipate a visit to the imperial eagles' terrain?'

CHAPTER TWO

DINNER was a strained affair. As if he had at last become conscious of the effort Dr Ribero and his staff had made to impress their honoured guest, the Conde kept a whip hand on tongue and temper and offered stiffly gracious comments about the *gazpacho*, a tasty cold soup with the tang of cucumber, and the *tortilla* that was served as a main course, an omelette filled with potato and onion, thick and cake-like, golden brown and crusty on the outside, soft and succulent inside, made to look colourful with the addition of tasty titbits Frances identified as peas, spinach, mushrooms, parsley, chopped ham, anchovies and even tiny pieces of sausage.

Dr Ribero apologised to her when the simple dessert was brought to the table. 'Spaniards invariably prefer to end a meal with fruit, *señorita*, but I know that you English are fond of puddings, therefore I asked my cook to prepare a caramel custard. I hope it is to your liking?'

'It's delicious,' she murmured, setting a seal upon her appreciation with a smile she hoped might cancel out the downcast look that had been caused by the peremptory manner in which the Conde had waved the sweet away. 'You run an extremely good establishment, Doctor,' she complimented, exercising the English virtue of always giving credit where it is due. 'The rooms are beautifully kept, the beds comfortable, and the meals—if the one we have just eaten is a fair example—are exceptionally good. In fact, considering the amenities and the services offered, I was surprised to discover that I'm your only guest.'

As she had intended, the doctor's worried look was replaced by a glow of pleasure.

'We are moving towards the end of our low season, *señorita*. Most of our guests arrive during spring and autumn when the marshes are crowded with birds that have travelled from as far away as the Tropics and the Poles. From the hot regions come the purple heron, the egret, the stork, and the bee-eater, as well as your English robin, the Scottish woodcock, the greylag goose on its way to Denmark, and the widgeon en route to Northern Siberia. During the wet season guests are transported through the marshes in punts drawn by oxen, but at this time of year when the warming sun is beginning to set the dried-out marsh bed hard as concrete we find that horses supply the best mode of transport.'

'The *only* form of transport,' the deeply brooding Conde corrected. Frances tensed, intuitively sensing that an awkward question was about to be directed her way. 'Tell me, Señorita Ross,' he did not disappoint her, 'are you accustomed to spending many hours in the saddle?'

'I have ridden before,' she gulped, made determined by the glint of mockery in his eyes that nothing would force her to admit that her solitary attempt to ride a horse had been a complete fiasco.

'In that case,' she thought the tight stretching of

his lips formed the unpleasantest smile she had ever seen, 'as you appear determined to flout both danger and convention, I can arrange to put one of my Arab stallions at your disposal.'

Her frightened heart leapt high into her throat, but mercifully, before her stunned mind could formulate an excuse for declining the offer, Dr Ribero leapt to her rescue.

'Don't worry, *señorita*,' he smiled, 'El Conde is obviously enjoying a small joke at your expense. His preference for highly bred, fiery-spirited steeds is so well known in this area that even I would think twice about mounting one of his high-stepping, temperamental thoroughbreds. But at least,' he continued slyly, 'you can take heart from the fact that El Conde's offer might be regarded as tacit acceptance of your right to remain in Andalusia in order to continue your quest for the information needed to conclude your father's book. The main breeding ground of the imperial eagle is situated on his land, the exact location is known only to himself and a few trusted members of his staff, therefore the success of your mission depends entirely upon El Conde's willingness to act as your guide. Without his permission, no one dare trespass on his land.'

Frances had to call upon every last ounce of courage in order to ride the bitter blow. The last thing she wanted was to remain in the company of the arrogant Conde, whom she was growing to dislike more and more with each passing minute. Yet the prize at stake was the finalising of a book which she knew in her heart was the best of any previously written by her father. Also, his ambition to conclude the book with a chapter devoted entirely to the rarest bird in Europe had been passed into her keeping, not as a mere legacy of duty, but as the means of attaining a personal goal—one crowded hour of glorious achievement!

With the threat of disappointment hanging over her head, it was not as difficult as she had imagined to keep her tone pleasant when the Conde began delving into her background with the thoroughness of a Spanish inquisitor.

'The fact that for the past couple of years you appear to have been content to act out the role of general dogsbody contrasts oddly with your views on female emancipation. But then,' he added with more than a hint of sarcasm, 'bathing in reflected glory requires far less effort than striving for academic qualifications of one's own.'

'Quite so,' she agreed evenly. 'However, I was fortunate enough to be able to reap the benefits of both worlds. I am a fully qualified teacher,' she tilted proudly, 'and once I've finished my father's book I intend searching for a post.'

She sensed his sudden stillness, saw his fingers stiffen and remain poised over a walnut as if his mind had been startled to sudden attentiveness.

'So you are fond of children?'

'Very,' she returned promptly.

Casually, he picked up the walnut and returned it to its dish, then with his eyes hooded, his expression guarded, he surprised her with the question:

'Would you mind explaining why?'

'Oh . . . for various reasons,' she faltered lamely, searching a mind rendered suddenly blank. Then, recalling times spent helping out in nursery schools during long summer vacations, the pleasure she had discovered in exploring personalities as individual and complex as any grown-up's, she decided simply, 'Mostly, I suppose, because of their joy in simple pleasures; their honesty and complete lack of guile, and especially,' she smiled with a faraway look in her eyes, 'because of the self-assurance they've gained from knowing that they are greatly loved.'

'But what if they should sometimes be dirty, noisy, and ill-behaved?' he probed as if anxious to hear her reply.

'Aren't they always?' She was actually able to laugh aloud. 'Some of the greatest pleasures of childhood are to be found exploring the depths of deep, dusty cupboards; in out-yelling companions, and in occasionally courting their admiration by tilting at authority. A torn dress can soon be mended, *señor*, but a child's heart, once it has been bruised, takes much longer to heal, which is why I disapprove strongly of punishing with harsh words.'

When he jerked his chair away from the table and rose to tower over her she felt certain that she had somehow managed to offend him. Fearfully, she looked up, her troubled grey eyes ready to plead, then remained transfixed by a smile as startlingly unexpected as the sight of sunrays splitting a heavy black storm-cloud asunder.

'Bernardo,' he addressed the equally surprised-looking doctor, 'please arrange to have horses and a small amount of provisions ready for our departure in the morning. Señorita Ross,' he turned to astound her breathless, 'might I suggest that you retire to your room immediately in order to get as much sleep as possible. Tomorrow, we have a long journey ahead of us, and provided you feel up to it I should like to set off shortly after sunrise.'

In spite of the fact that she was annoyed with herself for jumping to obey his command with such alacrity, Frances slept well and was astir long before the early morning call that informed her that El Conde was ready and waiting. She had even taken time before retiring to bed the evening before to sort out what she reckoned to be the minimum requirements for her excursion: a large exercise book in which to jot down notes, sponge bag, pyjamas, a change of underwear, a couple of spare shirts, a pullover, tights, socks, tissues and, just in case the journey could not be accomplished in one day and it might be found necessary to stay somewhere overnight, a black skirt made of knitted jersey that could be rolled up tightly without fear of creasing. The last thing she added to the pile which she was hoping might be accommodated within a couple of saddlebags was a plastic holdall divided into sections, containing moisturising cream, a small amount of make-up, lipstick, an eye-shadow palette, manicure set, needle and thread, Elastoplast, a comb, soap, and a tube of cream shampoo.

Immediately she began descending the staircase she saw the Conde pacing the hall. At the sight of the bundle she was carrying his eyebrows lifted slightly, nevertheless her outfit of slim, serviceable denims, checked shirt and lightweight anorak seemed to meet with his approval.

'You must be content with a breakfast of *tortas* and *café*,' he told her without the least hint of apology. 'Bernardo tried to insist upon arranging for kitchen staff to be on duty, but I'm sure you will agree that at such an early hour only the services of a groom are necessary.'

He plucked the bundle out of her nerveless fingers. 'Give that to me, I'll begin stowing your stuff inside the saddlebags while you are eating breakfast. I had mine more than an hour ago.'

Struggling to subdue an overwhelming shyness of the man who, wearing a *caballero's* grey riding suit and with a round, grey sombrero positioned over a chequered cloth designed to protect his neck from the sun, looked even more intimidatingly Berberish than he had the evening before, Frances nodded briefly, then sped towards the breakfast *salón* before he could spot flags of embarrassed colour driven into her cheeks by the thought of anyone other than herself handling her very personal possessions.

However, the looming prospect of an even worse ordeal took precedence in her mind, throwing her into such a state of anxiety that a gulped cup of coffee was all the breakfast she could manage. Nerved to a pitch of high tension, she strode outside the Palacio, then just managed to smother a tell-tale gasp of relief when, instead of the formidable Arab steeds she had been expecting, she saw a groom holding a couple of small but wiry-looking mounts equipped with what looked to be comfortably contoured saddles, high fore and aft, that had soft sheepskin seats which she felt certain she would find it almost impossible to fall out of.

A glance confirmed that the Conde appeared to have had no difficulty finding room for all her things inside two embossed leather saddlebags slung over the cantle and that he had even managed to accommodate a waterproof cape and a leather wine-skin within what looked like several pairs of leather bootlaces attached to the saddle.

Either her expression reflected her thoughts, or the Conde's dry observation was an indication of an uncanny ability to read her mind.

'The Arabian thoroughbred is unrivalled for speed, *señorita*, but these small horses of the sierras are ideal for travelling in rougher terrain. They are very strong, extremely surefooted, seldom go lame, and have rarely been known to stumble down even the stoniest mountain path. You are certain to be pleasantly surprised by their comfortable armchair canter.'

Offering up a silent prayer of thankfulness to whichever saint had been moved to work a miracle on her behalf, Frances accepted the reins of her placid-looking mount, placed her right foot up into a broad metal stirrup, then swung her left foot over until she was seated in the saddle. When she did not immediately fall off on the other side, she felt her show of courage had been amply rewarded.

'*Monte*! *Monte*!' the Conde urged. 'Get on! We have a long ride ahead of us!'

Keeping her mind blank, veering deliberately away from the memory of her previous attempt at horse riding that had lasted all of ten minutes,

Frances tightened her grip upon the reins, nudged her heels into the horse's ribs, and was lurched suddenly into motion.

For the first ten minutes she had to concentrate solely upon keeping her seat, trying to adjust to a bumpy, frightening method of transport that entailed being perched precariously above the ground, but as she became accustomed to the rhythm of her mount's stride she felt able to relax and began taking an interest in her surroundings.

Luckily, the Conde was riding a few paces ahead. After tossing in her direction a smaller version of the flat grey hat tipped to the back of his head with the terse instruction, 'Wear it, you'll be glad of its protection later in the day,' he had taken the lead and lapsed into silence, seemingly absorbed in thought. So she jogged contentedly in the rear, taking mental notes of an expanse of sun-cracked marsh bed, its flatness relieved only by clumps of tall grasses, and in the far distance humps of dun-coloured ground that Bernardo had referred to as *vetas*, stretches of land left dry even when the marshes were flooded that provided ideal foraging and nesting places for birds and small animals.

Her spirits rose as she began appreciating the pleasant ride in the comparatively cool morning air, but as the sun began gradually rising higher and higher she became conscious of the first small indications of discomfort—an ache in the small of her back, a stiffness in her joints, sweat that began as a trickle between her shoulderblades and then graduated to a flow that caused her shirt to cling like a sodden rag to her back.

After a couple of hours, just when she felt the edge of her endurance had almost been reached, the Conde twisted round in his saddle to indicate a spread of cork oak trees outlined upon the horizon.

'We'll stop there for a rest and a bite to eat.'

Feeling the quizzical scan of his eyes over her slumped body, she jerked erect and tried to avoid sounding as enervated as she was feeling.

'Good!' Much to her annoyance the solitary word erupted like a parched croak. Swallowing hard, she managed to enunciate the lie, 'Physically, I feel quite fresh, but I wouldn't say no to a drink.'

Her dislike of him escalated when a short, mirthless laugh told her that he was not deceived, that he might even be anticipating gaining a great deal of satisfaction from signs of her growing discomfort. Gritting her teeth, keeping her eyes fastened upon the goal shimmering like a mirage on the hot blue horizon, Frances travelled in his wake, hoping to keep hidden from his eagle-keen glance the punishment that every slight rise, every gentle dip, was inflicting upon her racked body.

As he had promised, she was grateful for the protection of the hat he had provided as the sun rose higher in a sky empty of all but soaring, swooping birds. Occasionally, a startled boar darted out of their path and herds of grazing fallow deer retreated nervously from the sight and sound of riders intruding into the immense solitude of the marshes.

Her relief when they finally arrived at their resting place was so great that she forgot the need for pretence and slumped down in the saddle, too

weary, aching and sore to muster sufficient energy
to dismount. But the living nightmare was
intensified when the Conde's horse, probably
startled by some small creature running across its
path, reared, at the same time letting out a startled
neigh that had the effect of a pistol shot upon
colonies of nesting spoonbills, herons and egrets
that rose screaming and shrieking from the trees to
hurl a chorus of raucous protest over the heads of
the interlopers. Instinctively, Frances reacted by
throwing her arms above her head, alarmed by the
obvious resentment of the viciously diving birds
whose powerfully flapping wings were blurring her
vision. Then suddenly, her senses confused by a
combination of heat, fatigue and fear, she
experienced a soaring sensation and felt herself
being lifted clean out of the saddle.

'No need to be alarmed, *señorita*, in a few
minutes the birds will settle on their perches and
soon afterwards you will be able to forget their
existence.' Then the Conde's glance sharpened.
'You look all in,' he accused, digging his fingers
into her waist as he bent to examine more closely a
wan face pinched with exhaustion. In a tone brittle
as threaded glass, he demanded, 'Tell me, Señorita
Ross, were you being truthful when you implied
that you were an experienced horsewoman?'

Daring to raise her eyes no higher than the third
button on his jacket, she gulped, 'I didn't claim to
be an expert, all I said was that I'd ridden before.'

'How many times before, and for how long?' he
pressed.

Quickly, her head drooped low as if she were
finding the weight of her grey Cordoba hat

unbearable. 'Once,' she admitted in a low whisper, 'and for just a few minutes.'

'*Madre de Dios*!' The exclamation hissed from his lips with all the venom of a snake rustling through dried leaves. 'Yet you dare aspire to become a teacher, to achieve the stature of a giant amongst pygmies, when you obviously lack even the modicum of intelligence displayed by infants whose first steps are always taken with caution!'

'I've always considered experience to be the best teacher!' she was stung to retort. 'Life is a succession of lessons whose roots can be bitter but whose fruit is more often sweet.'

Her heart almost stopped beating when she dared to meet the fiercely angry glare of the man who seemed to use an aloof, haughty manner to clamp down upon passions continuously simmering on the boil, permitting occasional hisses of steam to act as a safety valve in case of a sudden, scalding overflow. He provided proof of this theory by releasing his grip upon her waist, dismissing anger with an indifferent shrug.

'There is an ancient Eastern proverb that states: "A man's worst enemy cannot wish him worse harm than he imposes upon himself". All I ask, *señorita*, is that you refrain from complaining— verbally or otherwise—about your self-inflicted injuries.'

Looking suitably chastened, Frances sank down on to the waterproof sheet he had spread upon the ground and waited until he had unearthed from his saddle bag a flat, round crusty loaf into which he stabbed a *navaja*, before extending it towards her with a slice of bread speared on to the tip of the eating knife. She accepted with inner reservations, but when she bit into the off-white, unbuttered slice she was pleasantly surprised to discover that the slightly coarse textured bread tasted delicious, as did the cold *tortilla* that made up the total sum of their picnic.

As she sat silently munching, taking occasional swigs of water from the leather wineskin the Conde had detached from the laces on her saddle, her aches gradually began to subside, so much so that she eventually managed to summon up sufficient courage to face him.

He was sitting with one shoulder propped against a tree trunk, his head flung back and mouth open wide to receive a thin stream of wine spouting from a leather *porrón*. Her carefully rehearsed words were forgotten as she sat entranced watching the ripple of throat muscles beneath skin like oiled silk, tanned to a light shade of coffee. When the convulsive movements ceased she raised her eyes to his face, then blushed at the sight of winged eyebrows that seemed to be accusing her of staring.

'Would you care for some wine?' He offered her the *porrón*.

'No ... no, thank you, I'm not fond of it; I much prefer to drink water.'

'Or milk,' he decided, laconically labelling her a milk-and-water miss.

Deciding that she really could not afford to offend the man who was lord of the particular piece of land she wished to explore, Frances made a determined effort to appear friendly.

'Although I've no notion what made you change

your mind about agreeing to act as my guide to the eagles' eyrie, Conde, I am very grateful that you did.'

'Various reasons prompted my decision, one of which was to be able to add one more book to the excellent collection of your father's works already in my possession.'

Warmed by his obvious respect for her father's work, she blurted impulsively,

'I'm sorry that you and he were never able to meet. I'm certain that you would have liked him if ever you'd managed to get to know him well.'

'I feel I did know him well,' he surprised her by saying. 'Because we shared a mutual regard for his work, Dr Ribero was kind enough—with your father's permission, of course—to share with me the contents of letters which, as time progressed, graduated from sheets of ornithological data into an exchange of confidences between friends. In fact, the last letter we received informing us of the date of his arrival included his acceptance of my invitation to spend part of his visit in my home, the Palacio del Flamenco, that is situated conveniently close to the breeding grounds of the eagles whose habits he was anxious to study.'

'Palacio del Flamenco,' she mused thoughtfully. 'I've been studying your language, off and on, for the past two years, but not until I actually arrived in Spain did I realise the extent of the gaps in my knowledge. Am I correct in translating Palacio del Flamenco as "Palace of the Gypsy Dance", *señor*?' she puzzled with a frown. 'I feel intuitively that the name is inappropriate . . .'

'I know of many who would be prepared to

swear that female intuition is infallible,' he told her morosely. 'However, the very fact that you are here with me now must prove such a belief mere fallacy.'

Ignoring the rasp of her startled breath, he clipped precisely, 'The language of Spain, in common with that of your own country, has many words that have separate and entirely different meanings attached. As you correctly assumed, *flamenco* can be interpreted to mean "Spanish gypsy dance", but its alternative meaning is "*flamingo*" which as you are no doubt aware is the name given to the long-legged, flamboyant birds whose fluttering wings can cast a roseate haze over an entire flock before they sheath their wings and revert to their normal white sheen. On a lake in the grounds of the Palacio there are often up to a thousand flamingoes cramming the entire surface of the water. They are drawn to the area by the high salinity of the water which suits their requirements. Lately, however, the population seems to have been gradually dwindling.'

'Perhaps,' Frances choked, grappling to keep a rein on her mounting suspicion of the man whose motives she did not trust, 'they've merely decided upon a change of breeding ground.'

'Perhaps,' he shrugged. 'I doubt if anyone will ever know for certain. The migration pattern of flamingoes has never been investigated in depth; there is still a great deal of mystery surrounding these birds. However, what *has* been recorded—if only in legend—is the fact that flamingoes were using the lake as a breeding place when the first Moorish prince invaded Andalusia. Either from choice or necessity, he settled here and built himself a palace, intending to fill it with young Spanish concubines. However, contrary to Moorish custom, he took into his charge only one—the beautiful Isabella who later became his bride.'

'How horrible to have been forced into marriage with such a barbarian!' she shuddered, grey eyes dark with compassion for the long forgotten slave-bride. 'Had she no family, no father nor brothers to fight for her release?'

'Possession is nine tenths of the law,' he crisped, shading his eyes to look towards the sun, 'but as history has recorded that she gave birth to six fine sons, she must have been amenable to his advances at least some of the time! It was she who gave the Palacio its name. It is said that whenever she felt lonely, merely watching the flamingoes made her feel happy and contented again.

'Ah, good!' He peered into the sky with a look of satisfaction. 'Here comes the helicopter. No more questions for the time being, if you please, *señorita*, whatever else you wish to know you may find out for yourself once we arrive.'

'Arrive?' she questioned so faintly the word was almost drowned by the noise of rotor blades. Desperately, she cleared her throat and tried again. '*When we arrive where?*'

'At the Palacio del Flamenco,' he said implacably, 'where you will be staying for an indefinite period as my guest.'

CHAPTER THREE

IT hardly seemed credible, Frances thought dully, yet there was only one possible conclusion to be drawn from the Conde's words and actions. She had been abducted! Back home in England such a notion could have been treated as a joke, but this was Andalusia, an isolated, sparsely populated region where for centuries time had almost stood still, where the gospel of the Moors and their barbaric commandments still ruled. 'Possession is nine tenths of the law!'

Dazedly, she gazed out of the window at the fast receding ground. She had barely been given time to voice a protest. Indeed, she had been so shocked, her mouth so dry with fear, that it had taken considerable effort on her part to jerk out the reminder.

'Dr Ribero will be bound to raise an alarm if I don't return to collect the rest of my belongings within a reasonable space of time.'

The Conde had cast her a look that had seemed to war between impatience of her stupidity and sympathy for her innocence.

'Bernardo was pleased to have the responsibility for your welfare taken out of his hands.'

'You mean that he's aware of, and prepared to condone your high-handed action?' Frances had almost choked on her indignation. 'I'm sorry, but I find that impossible to believe—the

doctor impressed me as being the epitome of the
sort of chivalrous, honourable gentleman for
which Andalusia is renowned. He would never
allow——'

'Of course he would not,' the Conde had
brusquely forestalled her, 'so far as Bernardo is
aware you have eagerly accepted my invitation to
stay at the Palacio del Flamenco so that you may
study the Spanish imperial eagle at your leisure.
Why else do you suppose he fell in with my plan to
take you on a short tour of the Reserve of which
he is so proud, and why he even agreed to arrange
for the ponies to be collected from the spot where
we arranged to leave them grazing?'

'But why? Why are you doing this?' She had
stamped her foot in anger and frustration.

But in the manner of an imperious Moor he had
turned away, brushing aside her protest with the
same casual indifference he would have shown
towards a persistent sandfly.

'Make out to sea before setting a course inland,
Manuel,' she heard him instruct the pilot. 'I'd like
my guest to enjoy a bird's eye view of the whole of
the province.'

Frances was tempted to retort that she could
enjoy nothing in his company, that she resented, as
much as the beautiful young Isabella must have
done, being plucked like a sparrow into the talons
of an eagle and soared towards his isolated eyrie.
But some instinct warned her to hold a tongue that
would be bound to babble, spilling out the fear
welling up inside her, an emotion that robbed the
mind of all powers of reasoning and so had to be
suppressed, because never in her life before had

she been in so much need of a cool head and calm demeanour.

When the Conde left his place next to the pilot and clambered into the seat next to hers, it was as much as she could do to suppress a shudder. Nevertheless, when he touched her arm and nodded towards the window she followed his instruction to look downward.

'That strip of coastline you see below comprises the most desert-like shores of Spain. Miles of straight, smooth, deserted beach backed by a range of gigantic sand dunes that encroach inland for many miles.'

She craned her neck and saw brilliant blue sea lapping a white sandy shore devoid of all movement, without beach huts or parasols, without bathers or lines of oiled, half naked bodies marring its miles of virgin perfection. She blinked when the helicopter wheeled in the sky and began flying inland over a white sandy waste from which sun rays were bouncing a fierce dazzle.

'Soon, we will once again be passing over the Palacio de Rocio and afterwards the Reserve. Then once we leave behind the marshes through which we have travelled on horseback, we will begin heading towards the lofty range of the Sierra Nevada where, with its head resting against a background of snowy peaks and its toes dipping into cool green valleys, you will be privileged to catch your first glimpse of the Palacio del Flamenco.'

'As a prisoner is privileged by the first sight of his dungeon?' she rounded on him, sorely tried. 'As the young slave, Isabella, was privileged to be permitted her first glimpse of the cage inside which she had been condemned to live a lifetime? What do you *want* from me, *señor*?' Her yell was almost drowned by the noise of rotating blades. 'You've taken great pains to display the inaccessibility of the region in which you live, the impossible task facing any prisoner foolish enough to attempt an escape, yet I'm neither rich, important, nor am I beautiful, so what possible reason can you have for choosing to take *me* hostage?'

'Calm yourself, *señorita*!' The snapped command, the bite of his fingers into her wrist, acted like a douche of cold water upon her rising hysteria. 'Even when the atmosphere is conducive—which at the moment it is not—I never proffer explanations, have never before been expected to account for my actions. But as you appear to be convinced that you are about to be deprived of your obviously cherished virginity, I will set your mind at rest on that account. No, you are not rich,' he ticked off her first protest with a contemptuous flick of his finger, 'but even if you were, I doubt whether you would be able to outmatch the combined wealth of a Moorish prince and generations of Spanish conquistadors. To your second point I will respond only with a question: How is it possible to even contemplate equating one holding the title "Lord of the Land" with a seeker after importance? And as for your third point'—deliberately, he allowed his eyes to stray over the childish curve of her cheek, along a tender line of neck and shoulder, then lingered so long studying the effect of agitated heartbeats hammering inside her breast she felt the nadir of mortification had been reached, '. . . compared with the exceptionally high standards set by Andalusian women you cannot be considered a raving beauty—not even your colouring can be regarded as unusual amongst people who still show traces of their blue-eyed, blonde-haired inheritance from Moorish ancestors,' he spelled out with thin-lipped cruelty. 'Your only value to me lies in your talent as a teacher, and for that I am willing to barter. You seek access to the breeding grounds of the Spanish imperial eagle, Señorita Ross—I need a teacher who is capable of communicating elementary subjects to my children.'

So the Conde had a wife and a family of children! Suddenly the suspicions that had given rise to her agitation seemed comparable with those of a maiden aunt. Undoubtedly, she had been justified in kicking up a fuss about having her freedom curtailed in such an arbitrary manner, but arrogance appeared to be the very essence of the man who had become accustomed to having his wishes fulfilled with instant, blind obedience by inhabitants of a backward, isolated community who had dubbed him Lord of the Land.

When he left her to take up position next to the pilot, she sank back into her seat and tried to dispel her feeling of foolishness by concentrating her attention upon the Andalusian landscape over which they were flying. As if following instructions to provide her with the best possible view, the pilot was flying the craft low enough for its shadow to be cast like some gigantic monster capable of proceeding without check over deep blue

Mediterranean sea, miles of gigantic sand dunes, woods of stone-pines, a line of freshwater lagoons, stretches of sandy heathland, cork oak savannah, then finally the marshland Reserve where the Palacio de Rocio loomed seemingly near enough to touch, before fading from sight as rapidly as her hope of rescue.

'Take a good, long look, *señorita*,' the Conde twisted round in his seat to indicate the perimeter of the Reserve fast receding in their wake. 'In just a short number of years from now there could be no place left in Spain to accommodate birds of the wilderness.'

'Surely not?' she faltered. 'Aren't you taking a rather pessimistic view, *señor*? Your government, in common with my own, must have made plans to protect the environment?'

He frowned, lips twisting wryly as a general being forced to concede the superior strength of the enemy.

'Neither political pressure, pleading, nor appeals to common sense have managed to topple tourism from the top of my government's list of priorities,' he shocked her by answering. 'Many have fought to save the Reserve, not only for the sake of its inhabitants, but also to provide enjoyment and education for future generations. However, in spite of all protests, it now faces the threat of what some dare to term progress. A proposal is even now being considered to build a motorway around the perimeter of the Reserve in order to provide a better and faster route to the tourist resorts that are sprawled along the coast just to the north of here. Inevitably,' he shrugged, 'developers will move in to build a string of new beach resorts. Birds and animals that are sure to stray into these places will be shot, household pets left to roam will present danger to the wildlife, so-called bird-lovers will steal rare eggs, careless picnickers will set fire to dry heathland.'

'But surely something can be done to preserve the wilderness?' Frances appealed, looking stricken. 'Why not try enlisting the aid of men of international stature, eminent biologists and ornithologists, for instance—the combined influence of such men of different nationalities should go a long way towards preventing the Reserve from being destroyed!'

'All that, and much more, has already been done,' he dismissed morosely. 'Every piece of ammunition we possess has been thrown into the war against progress, yet we have been defeated, not by the urgency of man's need, but by a combination of greed and the lethargy of an uncaring society. However, the battle has not been entirely lost,' he concluded grimly. 'As long as it lies within my power to ensure it, one small part of Spain will remain unviolated—one piece of wild, untamed terrain shall remain a refuge for the Spanish imperial eagle!'

Frances stared at the back of a black, imperious head showing snow-white markings at each temple, at a glimpse of aquiline features stamped with lines of such primeval intent that she was moved to wonder whether his resolution was strengthened in the same way that an eagle was purported to renew his strength. Was the Conde so closely allied to the rare bird that he too could practise the rites of the ancient superstition that claimed: 'Every ten years the eagle soars into the "fiery region" and plunges thence into the sea where, moulting its feathers, it acquires new life!'

She stirred restlessly, irritated by her indulgence in such fantasy, yet in spite of her self-derision she was unable to rid herself of a feeling of being in close proximity with a creature so regal it had been adopted as an emblem of royalty, a creature used in heraldry to denote one who has been honoured with a charge of great responsibility.

The Conde left her to gaze in peace while they flew over valleys and plains abloom with tropical flowers, sometimes gently blending, at others combining to create explosions of yellow, red, purple and flaming pink against the heat-hazed landscape. On hillsides vines stood in serried rows and olive trees formed welcome groves of silvery green against dry red earth. Enormous ranches scattered with herds of huge black bulls stretched the length of river banks, and as they flew low over towns and villages she peered down at white houses built around courtyards filled with flowers, with windows decorated with the same black iron scrollwork as balconies where women leant gossiping, wearing black lace mantillas draped like shawls over their heads.

Many lovely buildings, their stone carved into a semblance of lace, passed under their shadow as they journeyed eastward, invading the privacy of patios where cool fountains whispered, causing much excitement amongst workers who stood gaping skyward as the noisy modern phenomenon disturbed the peace saturating groves of orange, olive, banana and prickly pear trees.

But then, like a reminder of home, a range of snow-capped mountains erupted across the skyline and shortly afterwards the craft began soaring above foothills towards what looked from a distance like a towering stronghold with ochre-coloured walls—a Moorish palace built for an Arab grandee!

'Welcome to the Palacio del Flamenco, Señorita Ross.' When the Conde turned around Frances saw that his face was gravely unsmiling. 'Some say that to live here in Andalusia is to be slowly born again, sometimes as a stranger totally unknown, completely different from one's normal self.'

She stared fixedly as they approached a fortress built in the very heart of nature itself, with the wild, rocky backdrop of the Sierra Nevada mountains, its summits still showing traces of snow, a foreground of gentle slopes scattered with shrubs burning in the sun, then a sweep of lush, cool valley filled with orchards where trees hung ponderous with fruit and terraced vineyards crept high up the sides of sunbaked hills nourishing a crush of tiny green grapes slowly approaching crisp, juicy maturity.

But it was not until the helicopter soared over thick, crenellated walls enclosing the extensive grounds of the Palacio del Flamenco and began hovering over a landing pad before descending surely as an eagle homing on to its nest that Frances began appreciating fully the extent of isolation achieved by his escapist retreat. It was a world within a world, a place where the noise and pressure associated with a society greedy for commerce did not exist, a place where peace waved a healing wand over taut nerves and a centuries-old blanket of silence descended over flower-massed, heavily perfumed gardens, stretches of lush, shaven lawn, paths that meandered through shrubberies, leafy arbours, and around fountains with huge stone basins containing plump goldfish gliding indolently beneath a canopy of waterlily leaves. It was as if, the moment the pilot had cut the engine, he had simultaneously cut off every last link with the twentieth century.

'As you will see for yourself very shortly, *señorita*,' the Conde directed her with a wave along the path he wished her to follow, 'the rear of the Palacio is not so Moorish in design as the frontal approach which has been kept as nearly as possible to the original building constructed by the founder of our family in the eleventh century. Over the years some concessions have been made to comfort.' Very conscious of his guiding hand upon her elbow, Frances quickened her steps to keep pace with his rangy stride as he hurried her past a swimming pool lined with tiles of such brilliant, shimmering blue she had to blink rapidly in an attempt to protect her dazzled eyes.

'The *maias*, or covered terraces, are typically Mauresque, however, as are the white marble floors, the horseshoe archways, and garden ornaments such as this which is one of several you will see scattered throughout the grounds.' With a wave, he indicated a Moorish oil jar so huge she had to tilt back her head in order to fully encompass its height.

'However, successive generations of Andalusian

brides have insisted upon adding refinements
scorned by sons of the desert but considered
essential appendages to comfort by the spoiled
daughters of Spain. Isabella, for instance, the first
young bride, was reputed to have rebelled against
her husband's bizarre practice of setting the skulls
of his enemies with jewels and then using them as
drinking goblets,' he informed her mildly, the
casual tenor of his voice at odds with the flash of
amusement in eyes scanning her scandalised face.
'No doubt she resented his persistent humbling of
the remains of her vanquished countrymen, and
set about employing feminine wiles to convert him
into a more charitable frame of mind.'

'And did she succeed?' Frances croaked, feeling
threatened by an ambience of such lingering
barbarity she would have been prepared to believe
that the helicopter now barely discernible in the
distance had transported her backward in time to
the savage era of the Moorish invasion of the
Spanish peninsula.

'Up to a point,' he nodded, his lips set
suspiciously firm. 'The Moor ordered the removal
of the jewels from the skulls, then had them
planted with flowers and set along the length of
the terraces with a name inscribed on each one so
that, when he strolled past enjoying the colour and
perfume of the varied bouquets, his mental words
of gratitude could be offered to the appropriate
donor.'

When at that precise moment they rounded the
side of the Palacio her loudly audible gasp was
caused by a combination of outrage aroused by
the lack of sensitivity shown by a prince who had

carried vindictiveness beyond the grave, and awed admiration of the mind that had envisaged and then supervised the construction of a frontage guaranteed to impose the insignificance of a flea upon any mortal possessing temerity enough to step within its shadow.

In spite of centuries of necessary maintenance the huge stone façade carved to resemble a curtain of fine lace appeared untorn, sweeping downward from a battlemented roof, past narrow arched windows bordered with white stuccoed embroidery of crescents and stars and tiny seashells, until it met a graceful marble arcade, its arches abloom with white plaster jasmine flowers climbing and clinging to delicate white mesh contrasting starkly beautiful against vivid, ochre-red walls.

Flowering downward from a massive door nourishing in its depths the hidden scars inflicted by the scimitars and lances of frustrated enemies was a tiered train of broad, shallow steps edged either side with marble plinths supporting statues of Egyptian gods of mythology, members of the family of Osiris, god of the Nile, who had been constantly at war with his family. Frances' stare became fixed upon profiles that looked vaguely familiar—some portrayed with the eagle-sharp beak and white-tipped feathered head of a predator, others with a ram's head surmounted by a solar disc, a few wearing the double crown of the Pharaohs but all, without exception, brandishing the flail and the sceptre used to denote the possession of supreme power.

She remained rooted, stunned by a feast of opulence her simple palate was unable to digest, a

vision of splendour that not even childhood
delving into the tales of Scheherezade had enabled
her to envisage. Shaken by her eruption into the
fabled past when Pharaohs who had been fond of
depicting the gods in their own images must have
posed to enable sculptors to chip a true, eagle-
eyed, fiercely-proud likeness out of stone, she
heaved a wondering sigh.

'What's wrong, *señorita*, you're looking extremely pale?'

If one of his petrified ancestors had spoken she
could not have been more startled.

'What?' She jerked violently and almost over-
balanced. 'Oh, nothing is wrong, *señor*,' she
gulped, easing her elbow free of his enquiring
touch. 'It's merely that I'm feeling completely
overwhelmed—all this,' she tried to encompass the
entire Palace of splendour within a weak wave,
'looks too fabulous to be real. It's like the
background for an Arabian Nights fairy tale, or
even a film set, an elaborately designed mock-up
that can be dismantled overnight and stored inside
a warehouse for future use.'

She could have bitten the unruly tongue that
had caused his look of cool disdain.

'Sometimes, *señorita*, I wonder how your race
ever achieved its reputation for diplomacy,' he
rebuked icily. 'Although the Palacio's original
structure may have been lost beneath the dust of
antiquity, I had nevertheless imagined, up until
this moment, that succeeding generations of my
family had managed to repair and restore the
Palacio to its former glory. Explore it at will,
señorita, I guarantee that far from discovering that

it is fashioned out of chipboard and balsa wood,
you are more likely to find that it owes its
durability to oak timbers salvaged from captured
English warships!'

The apology that leapt to her lips was stifled by
a gasp of surprise when the massive door swung
open and an elderly woman with bent frame and
wrinkled skin, yet with hair black as jet, hurried
across the threshold.

'*Bienvenido*, Romany Rye!' she cried out in
welcome, looking tempted to throw her arms
around the unbending Conde.

'*Gracias*, Sabelita,' he responded to the old
woman's greeting with a courteous bow.

Feeling a deepening illusion of having somehow
being roped in as an extra on a period movie,
Frances flinched from the probe of black button
eyes spearing countless questions in her direction,
wondering which position in the Conde's household was held by the obviously possessive, plainly
inquisitive old woman wearing a black dress with a
long, tightly fitting bodice and a full skirt frilled
from hip to hem that struck Frances as youthfully
incongruous on a woman of her advanced age. As
if starved of colour, she had also thrown around
her shoulders a small three-cornered shawl, heavily
fringed, and dotted with full-blown scarlet peonies,
and as if she was keen to draw attention to her dark,
glossy hair, golden earrings danced and dangled as
she moved to peer closely into Frances' startled face.

'*Bienvenido, chavali* . . .'

Much to Frances' relief the greeting sounded
encouraging, although she was able to understand
only half of it.

'*Chavali*?' she enquired with a tentative smile. 'I'm sorry, but that word appears to be missing from my vocabulary.'

'Romanies have no written vocabulary, *señorita*,' the Conde interrupted grimly. 'Sabelita welcomed you in Spanish, but it was in Romany that she addressed you as "girl" or "girl child". Sabelita was put in charge of the nursery on the day I was born. For some years, while I was absent from home attending boarding school and then later university, she returned to her tribe, but she seems to possess an uncanny instinct for knowing exactly when she is needed, for without giving me time to enquire about her whereabouts she appeared on the doorstep of the Palacio on the very day that I was deprived of the services of a housekeeper. I owe her a debt of gratitude, not only for her loyalty, but also, as Romanies are known the world over as inveterate wanderers, for remaining in one place much against her natural inclinations.'

Sabelita looked as pleased as a young girl receiving her first compliment.

'We Romanies do find the call of the wild irresistible,' she confirmed. 'Most of us are unable to keep still, to resist an inner urge to move on and keep moving, but we can be happy and contented if our surroundings are congenial. To label us vagabonds, as some have been known to do, is to do us great injustice, for we never go travelling without taking our homes along with us. And as for knowing when I am needed, Romany Rye,' she reproved the Conde gravely, 'you must be aware that I am known to possess the gift of second sight, that the gods send me direct information about future happenings. The gift is given to many, but only a handful are capable of correctly reading the signs.'

'Educated people refuse to be swayed by ancient superstition,' the Conde reproved sharply. 'Atmospheric conditions that cause comets to flame and stars to fall have been thoroughly investigated and explained by experts in terms simple enough to convince the majority of people that talk of evil portents is merely superstitious nonsense.'

Frances delved the depth of Sabelita's hurt when she saw a quiver disturb the calm serenity of her features, and championship of the old woman's brave spirit was reflected in her involuntary gesture of protest towards the sharp-tongued Conde. But surprisingly, Sabelita seemed to think that it was she who was most in need of comfort.

'Don't upset your kind heart on my account, *beti chavali,*' she almost intoned. 'Soon you will prove my gift of prophecy, soon—when my family is rejoicing at the wedding of our Bori Rani!'

CHAPTER FOUR

FRANCES stepped out of her bedroom and began walking along a gallery leading towards a staircase that climbed in broad flights from a large gloomy well, flanked by walls of coloured tiles reaching to the full height of a ceiling with a painted dome that was lost in the dusk of evening. What little she had seen of the interior of the Palacio had struck her as being only slightly less impressive than its façade. She loved her luxurious white and gold bedroom, the spaciousness of the galleries, the intimacy of the smaller salons, the cool comfort of internal courtyards supplying constant views of gardens bursting with colourful explosions of flowers so numerous their short-lived exuberance allowed for no empty gaps in the colourful display.

It was a palace built for escape, escape from the warm spring sunshine to which she had not yet become accustomed, escape from the noise of civilisation and, in the case of the aloof Conde, escape, she suspected, into a world where his word was law, where he ruled supreme over subjects who, if Sabelita was a true example, were devoted and fanatically loyal. Any further attempt to reason with the Lord of the Land, to argue with a man who felt it beneath his dignity to offer any explanation for his actions, would be a waste of time, therefore she had decided that all discussions

about her future would have to take place between
herself and his wife, the Condesa, she assured
herself, as she picked her way across the hall, loath
to set foot upon a mosaic floor depicting the three
stages of man's development—from birth and
childhood, youth and middle age, then final
senility—was bound to be more approachable,
more sympathetic to her argument that although
she was prepared to abide by the condition laid
down by the Conde, tutorage for his children in
exchange for the information she required, the
completion of her father's book had to be given
first priority, which meant that she could not agree
to stay in Andalusia for an indefinite period.

She jumped with alarm when a soft-footed
servant loomed out of the darkness, sheltering a
lighted taper behind his cupped palm. His flame-
flecked reflection struck her so grotesque she
almost screamed aloud, but after a quick mental
scolding she took a grip upon her nerves and
enquired politely:

'Would you kindly direct me to the dining *salón*
where I believe El Conde is waiting?'

Confidently expecting to make up the third
party of an intimate dinner *à trois*, she stepped
past the servant who had hurried in front of her to
open one half of tall double doors, then came to a
shocked standstill, staring around a *salón* as large
as a ballroom, with galleries running the width of
three of its walls and curved, Islamic arches giving
access to drawing-rooms and various other *salóns*
which, had a ball been in progress, could
comfortably have accommodated extensive buffets.
Running down the centre of the room, positioned

directly beneath a magnificent crystal chandelier, was a long table, its mirror sheen reflecting bowls piled high with fruit, silver candelabra, fine glass goblets and cutlery stamped with the eagle's head emblem of the Condes del Nomadas y Aquila ranged either side of lace table mats indicating places set for *two* people!

'*Buenas noches, señorita*! You found your room to your liking, I trust?'

Dazedly, she swung round in search of the owner of the voice and discovered the Conde looking formal yet relaxed in a white dinner jacket, dark slacks and a pastel-coloured shirt, its ruffled front and cuffs edged with a deep shade of blue embroidery. A diamond glittered in his cuff when he raised an arm to check the time on a watch snapped around his wrist with a band of platinum.

'Punctuality is obviously one of your virtues,' he commented without allowing a smile to disturb the stern-set symmetry of his lips. 'Would you care for an aperitif, or shall I instruct the servants to begin serving dinner immediately?'

Feeling a mortified blush rising to the very roots of her hair, Frances glanced down at her serviceable skirt and fresh but strictly functional blouse, then began backing nervously towards the door.

'I'm sorry, Conde ... I'm not properly dressed for dinner. Perhaps,' she pleaded with a breathless catch in her voice, 'I could have something served on a tray in my room?'

'Nonsense!' He brushed aside her protest, attempting no apology in spite of the fact that as her host, fully conversant with the inadequacies of her wardrobe, his manners were more to be faulted than her own. 'Sit down, please, *señorita*, having eaten next to nothing all day your appetite must be as voracious as my own.'

Egged on by hunger, agreeing wholeheartedly with the understatement, she advanced into the room, then hesitated, her brow wrinkling with puzzlement as she queried the two place settings on the table.

'I can appreciate the reason for your children's absence at this late hour, Conde, but what about your wife? Surely the Condesa will be joining us?'

'Questions, questions, and still more questions!' he clipped, once more showing his dislike of what he obviously considered to be her presumption. 'A good meal ought never to be spoiled with contentious conversation. Be seated, if you please, Señorita Ross.' Decisively, he pulled back the chair positioned to the right of his own at the head of the table. 'The omission of instruction in the art of dining well has left a lamentable gap in your education. I shall take upon myself the duty of remedying the omission by proving to you that one is able to think better, sleep better, even to love better, after dining well.'

As she was ravenous, and there was undoubtedly little to be gained from carrying the argument further, she dropped into the seat he had indicated with apparent meekness, mentally promising herself that come what may she would refuse to retire to her room that evening without gaining a full, concise, and detailed summary of her position.

The meal, served with formal elegance inside a dining *salón* with walls ornately decorated with bright mosaics in colours echoed in richly woven rugs scattered at random over a polished wooden floor, was eaten almost in silence. After the initial ceremony of dipping three fingers into a bowl of perfumed water, came the serving of food evocative of dark, sunless alleyways, the souks, and casbahs from which the superb cuisine had originated.

They began with *bstilla*, a juicy, crisp, sweet-sour pie made up of innumerable paper-thin circles of pastry layered between exotic fillings containing spices, sugar and pigeon meat, quickly fried and then slid directly from the pan to the plate to be sprinkled with cinnamon and sugar.

The Conde drank wine with each of the many courses, but Frances asked for a glass of cold milk to accompany the little almond-stuffed pastries she chose in preference to the semolina dish packed with raisins, currants and chopped, blanched almonds which the Conde chose as a dessert.

By the time the exotic, leisurely-eaten meal had ended she was feeling replete, contented, and much better equipped to launch the offensive that could no longer be evaded. She was idly dabbling in the warm, rose-scented water of a freshly-filled finger bowl when the Conde signalled that he, too, was satisfied by rising to his feet and suggesting courteously,

'Let's retire into the drawing-room where we'll be much more comfortable. Can I get you a liqueur, a coffee, or perhaps a glass of mint tea?'

Frances shook her head and rose with a contented sigh.

'I'll just finish my milk, if you don't mind.' When she reached out to pick up her half empty glass he cautioned sharply,

'Please don't, it will be brought to you in the drawing-room.'

'Oh, but——'

'Unless,' he chopped off her protest with an edge sharp as steel, 'you wish to offend my servants greatly?'

Swallowing the rebellious reminder that she was a working girl unused, as he obviously was not, to being waited upon hand and foot, she moved towards the archway leading into a room where low-slung copper lamps were throwing a soft glow over a woven carpet fitted into a square of white marble floor space, its fringe lapping the base of velvet-covered banquette couches ranged around three of the walls. She sank down on to a couch and felt immediately seduced by the wine-coloured embrace of upholstery soft as a bed of down and jewel-bright cushions exquisitely embroidered to match the tops of plump pouffes scattered around the floor, and curtains drawn together over windows running the height of the wall from ceiling to floor.

When a servant had placed her glass of milk and the Conde's baloon glassful of brandy on a beaten copper table set within easy reach, he silently withdrew, leaving her alone with his master, who appeared to be deep in thought, broodily contemplating the tip of a cheroot. The white-flecked wings of hair at his temples appeared startlingly pronounced as a beam of light played directly upon his bent head. Frances watched him closely, fascinated by the sharp-cut edges of a profile rapt with concentration, by a body that seemed relaxed but which, when goaded into action, could react with the tensile strength of a steel spring. Flame flared against the tip of the cheroot clenched between his teeth, then, bruising her vanity with the betrayal that he had almost forgotten her existence, he extinguished the flame and hesitated, his finger poised over the switch of an onyx table lighter.

'I beg your pardon, *señorita*, may I have your permission to smoke?'

The question was no more than a polite formality, of course. the Conde had made it plain that he considered himself possessed of a God-given right to do exactly as he pleased, nevertheless, Frances felt flattered by the unexpected act of courtesy.

'Please do,' her smile was a trifle wistful. 'I rather like the smell of tobacco. As a matter of fact, over the past months, one of the things I've missed most has been the rather pungent odour of my father's favourite pipe.'

'*Gracias*,' he acknowledged, setting a flare to her senses by choosing to sit so close that only the width of a narrow copper table lay between them.

Mentally registering relief at the thought that she was highly unlikely to be subjected to any stronger dose of a charm which she instinctively sensed could be deadly, she reached for the glass of milk that looked as incongruously out of place as she did herself, subconsciously emulating the superstitious followers of Islam who wore amulets and believed that immunity from all sorts of disaster could be achieved by clutching at talismans whenever danger threatened.

Unfortunately, her calm, sensible approach somehow deteriorated into a grab that jerked the glass sideways, spilling its entire contents over the Conde's immaculately tailored trousers.

'Oh!' Her round-mouthed gasp projected an amount of horror hugely disproportionate to her crime. 'I'm dreadfully sorry, I'm not usually given to being so clumsy!'

Frantic with dismay, she pulled a tissue out of her pocket, intent upon trying to diminish the damage, but he stayed her hand, fastening a grip upon her wrist that felt gouging as a talon.

'No, you are not usually clumsy, señorita,' he agreed. 'On the contrary, you are typical of your race, as cool, wholesome and sensible as the drink you seem to favour. Leave it!' he snapped, when she resisted his pressure in an effort to lever the tissue downward to mop up the spillage. 'What little damage has been done can easily be put right. Excuse me for a moment, if you please,' when he rose to his feet and released her hand blood began racing through veins dammed by the pressure he had exerted upon her wrist, 'I will return very shortly.'

When he had left the room she sat miserably pondering upon the mishap which normally she would not have allowed to happen. But since she had first set foot inside the palace built by a Moorish prince for his favourite concubine, her usually serene composure had been completely routed. Never in her life before had she experienced an atmosphere so laden with luxury, an El Dorado of wealth ruled by a man who, in common with the fabled king of that gilded city, seemed incapable of tasting the fiery tang of pleasure, appeared to have no one to guide him gently, and with love, towards the enjoyment of simple things.

She was musing upon the non-appearance of his wife, the elusive Condesa, when a movement caught her eye, drawing her attention towards a figure standing motionless, arms folded like wings across his chest, framed within the curve of a connecting archway. She caught a sharp breath, wondering for a second if she were in the presence of a princely apparition—a Moorish ghost whose heart had been so filled with love for his Isabella that he had offended against both custom and tradition by promoting a concubine to the proud status of Princesa.

The tall figure, stranded in the shadows beyond the perimeter of light being cast by low-slung lamps, seemed to be attired in the sort of loose white ankle-length garment favoured by sons of the desert who sought refuge from daytime heat and the chill of night-time within its voluminous folds. But when the figure moved closer towards the orbit of light Frances realised that it was no ordinary robe but a garment fit for a prince, with a heavily embroidered yoke, a clasp fashioned to resemble two golden claws, and a shower of multi-coloured stones scattered like raindrops over silk-petalled flowers.

'No need to look so startled, *señorita*. As any Arab nomad will confirm, the burnous is a comfortable, functional garment, extremely conducive to an evening's relaxation.'

She shuddered from the shock of hearing the Conde's cultured voice issuing from the figure she felt would not have looked out of place leading a cavalcade of warriors with banners flying, pulling impatiently on the bridles of Arab thoroughbreds so that their necks arched proudly as they cantered homeward with trophies of battle dangling from their saddle bows. With the stride of a forceful Moor he advanced to peer down into her frightened face. She backed away, then was made to feel foolishly ingénue when he chided dryly,

'What scandalous thoughts seethe behind your manner of prim decorum—a fine, sleek pelt denotes the hunting prowess of a well-fed beast, is that what you are thinking, *señorita*?' His jeering laughter scraped a permanent scar across her youthful sensitivity. 'Put your mind at rest, tonight the beast does not prowl, his mind is too set upon affairs of family to spare time for thoughts of ravishment!'

'I'm pleased to hear it,' she snapped as crisply as she was able, considering she was awash with embarrassment from head to toe. 'Believe me, *señor*, you would not have found me half so amenable to abduction had I not been consoled by the knowledge that you have secreted somewhere in the background of your life a wife and a family. How many children do you have, *señor*, and are they sons, or daughters, or both?'

Resuming his seat on the couch next to her, he reached for his glass and savoured half of its contents before startling her rigid.

'I made no mention of a wife, *señorita*, nor of sons or daughters—nevertheless, members of my family can be numbered in hundreds.' Edged almost to the brink of a smile by her wide-eyed stare of astonishment, he returned his glass to the table and continued with an air of resignation she found unforgivable, 'It is a long story, but as you will no doubt insist upon hearing all of it, I'd better start by explaining the implications contained within our family name. El Conde del Nomadas y Aquila is the title coined for the first Conde when he built the Palacio many centuries ago. "Count of the Nomads and of the Eagles",' he translated, 'an appropriate choice when you consider that there is no other place on earth where either species can hope to gain the protection they have always received on this estate. The Spanish imperial eagle was most probably breeding here long before the Moors arrived, but the appearance of the *nomadas*, or *gitanos*, as they are often referred to in Spain, coincided with a particularly vicious scourge being perpetrated upon their race by an unfeeling society. Harassed, persecuted, and made victims of unfair discrimination, one tribe appealed to the Moorish Prince for protection and was permitted by him to remain on a part of the estate that is honeycombed with caves which they utilised as homes into which the tribe settled and has remained up until the present day.'

'Do you mean that the family you spoke of is a tribe of gypsies?' She could not suppress her indignation at being so misled. 'And are you seriously expecting me to take up a post as teacher to such people?'

When his head snapped up she shrank from dark, Oriental eyes flashing a warning to take care, but felt stripped as an oyster of its shell when he bit out the sharp condemnation:

'You make it obvious by your tone, *señorita*, that you are as prejudiced as the majority of society towards the gypsy race. In every country, and by every nationality, they are used as scapegoats. For centuries they have been branded rogues, wherever they have travelled people have hated and envied them simply because they have always refused to conform to other people's values, because they have insisted upon remaining different by retaining their own tribal trades, language and customs. Yet in spite of the fact that their contempt of worldly goods has made them appear poor in the eyes of a mercenary society, it is a well established fact that they set standards—especially of morals and integrity—that are far higher than most. Unfortunately, what often seems to happen is that the arrival of gypsies in an area is welcomed by local criminals who tend to step up their unlawful activities, knowing that the *gitanos* will be blamed.'

The flaring of aristocratic nostrils, the tinge of temper on high cheekbones, confirmed his partisanship of the gypsy race far more than his terse yet impassioned spate of words. But to have referred to them as his *children*, to have implied that he was some kind of honorary gypsy chieftain, seemed to her to be a case of taking the duties of inherited patronage far beyond the bounds of what had originally been intended.

'I cannot pretend to be an authority on gypsy

law,' she responded coldly, 'however, their well-known contempt of those whom they choose to term "outsiders", together with their insistence upon living in exclusive, tightly-knit communities, must bear out the truth of the statement that "a person is gypsy only by right of birth".'

She saw his slight flinch, noted the tightening of lips which, in one less arrogant, might have been taken as an indication of pressure upon a sensitive nerve, but spurred on by anger caused by the suspicion that she had been deliberately misled, she continued to argue,

'In my own country, education authorities have been forced to conclude that gypsy children, because of their nomadism and an inability to adapt to the discipline of timetables and the need to remain quiet for long periods, are almost impossible to educate.'

'Exactly!' he pounced like a hungry eagle prepared to peck holes in her defence. 'What usually happens is that teachers relegate gypsy children to the bottom of the class and leave them to shift for themselves, easing their consciences by arguing that they are a disruptive influence upon the rest of the pupils, that they fidget, that they are noisy, dirty, and even that they are inclined to be rude. Those are precisely the reasons behind my decision to bring you here, Señorita Ross. I want you to establish the sort of school that can be held up as an example to other countries, where lessons take place in the open air, where impositions are kept to a minimum and rules are adapted to suit the freedom-loving natures of young *gitanos*. For too long the gypsy race has been deprived of the benefits of education! Its children must be taught how to count, to multiply and subtract, and to read and write—things that are necessary, if not to integrate them completely into modern life, then at least to allow them to handle themselves with more ease and to prove to the world that they are capable of better things than merely singing, dancing and playing the guitar!'

Sensing the danger of allowing him to detect any sign of weakness, Frances suppressed a shiver of alarm caused by the implication contained in his words. He appeared to be measuring her stay in Andalusia in months—perhaps even years!

Managing to muster a note of authority, she stated flatly, 'I'm sorry, Señor Conde, but even if I were prepared to embark upon such an assignment, which I definitely am not, the difficulties that would arise from my inability to communicate with the children would prove insurmountable. As you must already have gathered, my knowledge of your language leaves much to be desired——'

'But will improve rapidly with day-to-day conversation,' he interposed swiftly.

'. . . Also,' she continued doggedly, ignoring his interruption, 'though possessed of all the necessary qualifications, I've had very little actual experience of teaching. No,' she rejected the plan with a shake of her head, 'the sort of person you ought to be looking for is a mature, well-qualified teacher capable of casting a mantle of authority over any classroom, someone who is in sympathy with your aim to plant seeds of learning in the minds of gypsy children and who would be prepared to remain in Andalusia for as long as it may take to nurture tender shoots towards mature fruition.'

'That is exactly the type of teacher I do not want!' Prisms of light speared from the jewelled cloak disturbed by the irritated shrug of his shoulders. 'Such an experiment has been tried and failed, because of the *gitanos'* resentment of any stranger attempting to exert authority. The very fact that you are so obviously of a meek and mild disposition will weigh heavily in your favour,' he assured her with a note of finality that fell like a leaden fetter upon her last hope of freedom. 'Don't worry too much about the language barrier,' he encouraged almost kindly. 'Gypsies have their own basic tongue known as Romani, but the tribe whose children you are to teach— because it has remained so long under my family's protection—has little by little grafted so many Spanish words on to its own idiom that even local farmers find it easy to communicate. Provided,' he amended with a frown, 'the gypsies are disposed towards feeling friendly. If they should not be so inclined, they revert to their own secret code of communication that ranges from drawings traced in dust to knots twisted in the branches of bushes, a custom taught by Eastern ancestors who were parents to a culture born unknown centuries ago.'

Becoming suddenly impatient of the subject, he drew deeply on his cheroot, then stubbed it into a handy ashtray.

'Can I take it that the worst of your fears have been laid to rest, *señorita*, and that you will now cease worrying about children who pick up words as quickly as pigeons pick peas?'

Pride reared against the unmistakable note of dismissal in his voice.

'I have made plain my unwillingness to undertake such a task,' Frances retorted quickly, 'yet you speak as if my acceptance were a foregone conclusion.'

'It is—if I wish it to be!' Swiftly, he rose to his feet so that the loose white garment billowed like wings around his towering frame. '*And I do so wish!*' he stressed, baring white teeth in a humourless smile that made her feel weak and powerless, cowering as a sparrow in the shadow of a Spanish imperial eagle.

CHAPTER FIVE

'*Droboy tume, Romani chi!*'

Frances responded with an uncertain smile to what was obviously a traditional Romany greeting.

'*Gracias*, Sabelita,' she replied in Spanish. 'I shall have to ask El Conde to lend me a Romany dictionary so that I can extend the courtesy of replying in your own language.'

'*Nais tuke* is the usual response to such a greeting, *señorita*,' Sabelita beamed, 'but you will not find it written down in any book. Those of us who are still able to speak a complete Romanes are determined to ensure that the language, though secret, is not allowed to die out—that way, whichever countries of the world my people choose to visit they will be able to converse freely with members of their own race.'

She moved around Frances' bedroom, flicking a cloth at imaginary specks of dust, twitching curtains, moving an ornament here, a flower vase there, taking surreptitious peeks into drawers and wardrobe, making no secret of her disappointment with their contents. During the twenty-four hours that had elapsed since Frances' arrival at the Palacio, Sabelita had adopted a role that was a mixture of self-appointed protector, servant, friend and voluble informant on every subject, ranging from meals currently being prepared in the kitchen to details about El Conde's behaviour as an infant, as a tragically orphaned schoolboy, as a reckless adolescent up until—though Frances suspected that her revelations at this stage owed much to supposition—the present-day man whose aloof, forbidding manner she claimed could be blamed entirely upon too much solitude and the absence from his life of a devoted, loving wife.

Conscious that she was being highly honoured to share such confidences and that the old woman's absorption with the subject of El Conde was motivated by an almost fanatical devotion to the individual who had been placed in her charge minutes after his birth, Frances had made only feeble attempts to stem the flow of intimacies, nevertheless, a further succinct statement from Sabelita jolted her towards the realisation that the old woman's imagination was being allowed to run riot.

Flinging the door of a wardrobe open wide, she stared aghast at the oddments of shirts and denims spread out among the hangers and exploded wrathfully,

'Wearing clothes such as these, how can you hope to attract the interest of our Romany Rye! Where are the colours to draw his eye as a bee is drawn into the heart of fiery petals? Where is the plunging cleavage, the slit seams, the hip-hugging skirt designed to tantalise and excite a man until his senses reel? Where are the crimson and orange shawls, the gold bracelets and earrings to make music that will jangle in his ears long after he has ceased dancing? You have been blessed with the grace of a fawn,' she swung on her heel, black eyes

accusing, 'with immature curves holding a promise
of voluptuousness, with a skin matt as cream,
pale and pure as the milk men choose in preference
to wine whenever they feel a desperate need to
slake their thirst—so why do you hide the vivacity
that is the gift of women behind the gravity of
clothes that should only be worn by boys?' Her
wave encompassed every despised article of
clothing contained within the wardrobe. 'El
Conde's nature tends towards impatience, he
craves the novel, he is bored by the familiar, yet all
that is needed to drive the devils out of his heart is
the companionship of an attractive, adoring wife.'

Shocked to the core by the impassioned tirade,
Frances remained mute, then had to subdue an
impulse to laugh the old woman to scorn by
reminding herself that because of her age her mind
could be confused, even a trifle unbalanced.

Quietly, she attempted to ease her back on to an
even keel by reminding her, 'I met El Conde for the
first time only two days ago, Sabelita. I have no
designs upon him nor, I'm certain, has he upon
me. I simply cannot imagine what has led you to
believe otherwise. Try to think reasonably,' she
urged gently, 'ask yourself why El Conde, who
could probably choose a bride from a dozen
beautiful, eligible, highly-bred Andalusian girls,
should cast so much as a glance in my direction.
I'm sure the commonsense answer to that question
will be that such a notion is impossible.'

'Not so,' Sabelita shook her head with a
solemnity that caused Frances a tiny spurt of fear.
'It is written in the stars, in the sand and in the
movements of the planets, that you and Romany

Rye will take the bread and the salt.'

Feeling desperately ill at ease, Frances moved across to the window, trying to concentrate her mind upon a superb view of the Sierra Nevada and the green, well cultivated valleys sweeping down below the foothills; and at the gardens of the Palacio lying directly below, where curved stone archways were smothered in vines, where in ceramic-tiled patios the fruits of lemon trees were ripening in tubs and nearby fountains were arcing water endlessly from the mouths of birds, mammals and cherubs on to lily leaves floating on a surface of water that once might have reflected the dark, Oriental features of the Moorish prince and his young bride.

Feeling ill equipped to argue further with the old gypsy who seemed so certain of her ability to foresee the future, Frances seized upon curiosity as an excuse to change the subject.

'What do you suppose the Principesa looked like?' she pretended to muse aloud. 'Was she dark or fair, slender or well endowed, meek-natured or high-spirited? Whatever her looks, she must have possessed charm in abundance if, as legend would have us believe, she was able to sway the mind of her Moorish master away from thoughts of slavery and to persuade him to fly in the face of ancient taboo by elevating a lowly slave girl to the status of an aristocratic bride.'

'Isabella was a vision of female loveliness, with eyebrows that resembled picture clouds and arched over like a fighting cockspur; a nose like an opening jasmine bud, a neck with a triple row of dimples, a head like a bird's egg, and lips like the fissure of a pomegranate,' Sabelita almost intoned. 'Such abundance of beauty could not fail to attract the Moor's roving eye, but it was never his intention to make the young Isabella his bride, he meant merely to hold her captive until her attractions began to wane. But fetters of gold are still fetters to a gypsy girl whose spirit can be charmed but never tamed. So it fell to the lot of the elders of her tribe to reverse the position, to secure her release from bondage by turning master into slave.'

Frances turned away from the window, intrigued yet inclined to be sceptical. 'According to El Conde, the gypsy tribe appealed to the Moor for protection against harassment, persecution and unfair treatment, so its members would hardly be in a position to exert pressure upon a man wielding power and influence, even if he had become enamoured of a beautiful gypsy girl. But then,' she shrugged, 'time is a noted distorter of fact into fiction, and it did all happen a very long time ago.'

'The flamenco does not lie!' Sabelita cried out, obviously incensed. 'Flamenco stories are passed on by word of mouth from father to son—storytellers are keepers of gypsy history, they record our migration from the East centuries ago, help to preserve our traditions and our culture by chronicling the day-to-day lives of our people. Many of us cannot read or write, but our music is something that does not have to be written down, it expresses all our frustrations, our hopes, our fears, and it is the single most important bond that holds all gypsies together, not only in Spain, but all over the world. Were it not for flamenco, the tale of how our tribe—to which the young Isabella belonged—cast spells potent enough to draw down the moon, and concocted magic love philtres which were stirred into her master's drinks until he became besotted enough to make a barefoot gypsy slave girl his bride would never have been recorded! Were it not for flamenco, we would never have known how the Moor was persuaded into agreeing that his firstborn male child should be given the name Romanes, in case he should ever be tempted to forget that he had fiery gypsy blood racing through his veins, and also to act as a reminder to his gypsy family how greatly favoured it is to have as its chief a Romany Rye, a true gypsy gentleman!' she interpreted triumphantly.

Romany Rye! Frances jolted with surprise, realising for the very first time the significance of the name often used by Sabelita when addressing the Conde. So the first Condesa de Nomadas y Aquila had belonged with the gypsies! But surely the genetic strain could now be considered extinct, dissolved into oblivion by generations of aristocratic breeding? Or had it thrived, even been strengthened by some means known only to a race of nomads whose roots were buried deep within the bowels of the mystical East, a place of soothsayers and superstitious beliefs; of fakirs, hermits, taboos and sacred cows; of firewalking and levitation that confounded human logic; of mystic rites performed to placate the gods, of amulets and blue beads worn to act as a safeguard against the 'evil eye'?

She swallowed hard. 'Your tribe is fortunate to

have El Conde as its patron, Sabelita,' she frowned doubtfully, 'and he has made obvious the strong natural affection he feels for your race. Nevertheless, I am surprised by your eagerness to claim kinship with one whose measure of gypsy blood must now be minimal.'

With anxious eyes she quizzed Sabelita's face, hoping that the old gypsy woman would not take offence, then found herself wavering between surprise and relief when she read complacency in her smiling features.

'The truth of my claim is visible to all with eyes to see,' she asserted with a proud toss of her head. 'Each generation has been blessed with a Conde endowed with eagles' wings—the silver-tipped markings inherited from the first Condesa and shared by descendants of her family right up until the present day—that proves beyond doubt that he is one of us!'

Frances retreated from her bedroom, and with Sabelita's triumphant cackle still ringing in her ears made her way downstairs towards the courtyard at the rear of the Palacio from where the Conde had despatched a servant with a message requesting her presence.

She found him leaning with one shoulder propped against a trellis, his head tipped backward as he studied the height of the mountain above the tree line where a wilderness of grey rock, precipitous paths and melted snow streams bordered by purple irises and blue periwinkles began. When he remained unaware of her soft-footed approach she paused to inhale deeply the sweet, fresh aroma of springtime that was spreading a mantle of green over the lower slopes, coaxing fig leaves and mulberry leaves to open, and sticky poplar buds to unwrap in preparation for the arrival of the swallow, the cuckoo and the melodious nightingale.

As if becoming suddenly conscious of her presence, he swung round with a courteous greeting on his lips.

'*Buenos dias, señorita!* I hope you slept well and that you are feeling sufficiently rested to join me in a stroll around the gardens. Not far from here, within the boundaries of my estate, is situated the lake of the flamingoes, a spectacle which I'm certain you will find both exciting and amusing.'

Warily, she eyed the tall frame looking utterly relaxed in a short-sleeved sports shirt, open at the neck to show the swing of a golden medallion, and casual, lightweight slacks. The previous evening he had seemed surrounded by an aura of Oriental authority, this morning, with Sabelita's words still running through her mind, she imagined she could sense an air of amused tolerance that left her feeling shy and inexplicably tonguetied.

'Thank you, I'd like that very much,' she finally managed to mumble. 'If you don't mind waiting just a couple of minutes, I'll slip upstairs to get my camera.'

'Don't bother,' he brushed aside her request, 'the flamingo lake affords such a spectacle of colour and grace that over the years my study has become crammed with shots taken from every conceivable angle. You are welcome to take your pick. But perhaps you would like a coffee before we set off, or a cool drink, perhaps?'

'No, nothing for me, thank you,' she assured him hastily, anxious to avoid having to exchange polite social chitchat with the imperious, eagle-eyed Spaniard.

'Very well,' he looked relieved, 'in that case, *señorita*, permit me to lead the way.'

For a while they walked in silence along paths meandering through extensive grounds filled with flowers and freshly blooming shrubs which she knew, back home in England, would still be lying dormant, their leafless, frost-burned branches as yet untipped by buds of springtime green. The sun fell warm upon her shoulders, warning that later in the day its heat would burn like a scorch upon skin protected to the pale sheen of milk by scarves and jumpers worn as a defence against thin, icy winds. The air hung still and heavily scented, yet an impression of coolness was achieved by the sound of running water that was never out of earshot, water spouting into fountains, tumbling in streams down the side of the mountain, springing straight from deep underground fissures and caverns where it had seeped after trickling down from snow-tipped peaks, welling from underneath rocks to form deep still pools.

'I had imagined, *señor*,' she was moved to sigh, 'that the whole of Spain was a barren, parched plain. Nothing I'd read had prepared me for this ... this,' she waved an encompassing hand, 'green and pleasant oasis of fertility.'

He checked his stride, seemingly too absorbed in thought to assimilate the meaning of her words, then comprehension dawned as a glimmer of appreciation in his dark eyes, in the faint hint of a smile playing around the edges of a gravely-set mouth.

'We are blessed with an abundance of water,' he agreed. 'During winter it is left to flow into the ravines, but in summer it is fed into channels, some to maintain a constant supply to the villages, the rest being used to irrigate the valley.'

'Yes, you are fortunate,' she confirmed a trifle shyly. 'I would count myself lucky to see daffodils blooming in my garden back home, yet here apricots and persimmons are ripening and even orange trees are bearing fruit.'

'But our winter can also be cold,' he reminded her, his lips twitching slightly when she looked unconvinced. 'Believe me, there are some months of the year when I shun large areas of the Palacio and confine myself within one small *salón* that can be heated by a fire fuelled by small oak logs brought down from the mountains. Nevertheless,' her look of faint derision forced him to concede, 'in spite of autumn winds that seem to blow and blow, I suppose that, compared with your English winters, ours are relatively mild.'

They continued walking in companionable silence through a grove of chestnut trees ringed like a setting around a jewel-hued garden, the Conde guiding her around patches of soggy moss, indicating with a nod or a pointing finger a nest with an unidentifiable clutch of chicks bobbing above its rim, the darting progress of a colourful lizard, the wheeling grace of an eagle circling above the open canopy of overhead leaves.

Speech was superfluous, yet Frances felt that the silence he had imposed upon them was meant to serve some purpose. This suspicion was confirmed when a peculiar, monotonous grumbling sound fell faintly against her ear, then began gradually to swell, louder and louder as if, she thought, they were approaching some unseen, resentfully muttering crowd. She darted a look of enquiry towards the Conde, but with an inscrutable smile he waved her onward. Obediently she responded, her puzzlement growing as step by step the noise grew louder yet remained completely indistinguishable from any other sound she had ever heard.

Ten minutes later, when they stepped out of the trees into a huge clearing, she was hit by the impact of the most unusually beautiful bird spectacle she had ever seen. A few hundred yards from where she stood rooted, the waters of a lake seemed to be rippling beneath a mysterious white eiderdown hovering above a forest of long, thin stilts. She blinked, doubting the wisdom of her eyes, then as the Conde urged her forward the floating white mirage materialised into a vast flock of flamingoes nestling neck to neck, bustling, surging, jostling for position on long, stiff spindly legs jutting above the surface of the water. Busily, with heads bent low, they were sifting with their beaks through shallow water in search of food, too intent upon foraging to notice that they were being observed.

Gradually, the Conde guided her nearer to the white fringe of birds at the water's edge. Too near. Suddenly, a collective alarm alerted the entire flock and as they riffled their wings, preparing to take flight, the colour of the levitated eiderdown of feathers changed from white to brilliant pink. For breathless seconds the entire lake seemed to shimmer beneath a vibrant, roseate haze. Squawking and croaking their indignation, the flock floundered in panic, but when she and the Conde began backing away the shy, sensitive birds stopped fluttering and slowly sheathed their wings until the wave of colour faded and the flock turned white again.

They had retraced their steps far into the grove of chestnut trees before she managed to find words to thank him.

'I'm grateful for the privilege of being allowed to see such a beautiful sight, *señor*,' she tendered simply, sensing that he would resent effusive praise or expressions of delight which, however genuine, would still be inadequate.

'The privilege was mine, *señorita*,' he assured her gravely. 'Seeing the flamingo lake through your eyes was comparable to seeing it again for the very first time. What saddens me most is the thought that there will be few wild breeding places left in the world for our children to see, or our children's children. Almost certainly they will be denied the pleasure of seeing birds flying free, of watching animals in their natural habitat, not locked inside cages or confined within the perimeter of high wire fences. Which is why I consider it so important that you should complete the final chapter of your father's book, which at present some might praise on the grounds of literary merit, but which in the future will probably be looked upon as an invaluable tome of natural history.'

Frances flushed with pleasure and forgot to be shy of the noble Conde when, digressing from the well-trodden path, he took her hand and began leading the way along an overgrown path branching off into a tangle of undergrowth. Carefully protecting her face from thorns, sweeping whiplash branches from around her bowed head, he forged his way into a small clearing and rewarded her unquestioning obedience with the sight of a miniature cataract splashing into a pool of water so pure and clear that she could see white pebbles gleaming in its depths and slender strands of waterweed falling and rising, swaying and twisting, as if enjoying a slow, languorous dance.

Rooted in an overhang of rock were clumps of maidenhair fern and a few bushy plants with pale green leaves and a small white flower which, she noticed immediately she sat near, was emanating a scent so strong that the clearing seemed permeated with its heady perfume.

'This secret pool cannot be easily located until the *albahaca* is in bloom,' the Conde confided, reaching out to pluck a leaf which, when he crushed it in his palm, introduced into the air a different, aromatic smell that reminded her of the scent of sweet basil. 'The Moors were reputed to have. brought this herb from India where it is sacred to Krishna, and although it is used every day by wives in their kitchens, its flower is regarded as a symbol of devotion. To the gypsies, it has a special place and meaning in their love rites.'

For no obvious reason Frances blushed, then started with surprise when he stated with an uncharacteristic trace of whimsy,

'The *albahaca* and yourself appear to me to

share a common characteristic, *señorita*.'

'You mean because we are both small, pale and inconspicuous, *señor*?' she tilted, compressing her lips to disperse a quiver disturbing her hurt mouth.

'Certainly not.' When he shook his head, her pulses leapt into vigorous life, causing a sense of confusion that caused her to wonder whether the overpowering scent possessed magical properties that were affecting her reason. 'I was referring to the locally-held belief that the *albahaca*, *"Gently handled, will give a pleasant response, but if hardly wrung and bruised it will breed scorpions "*.'

She stared, nonplussed, wondering whether the lazily-proffered statement could be construed as an olive branch or as an exercise of derisive wit, then was forced to discount her suspicion of mockery when, instead of brutally demanding, he broached the subject of her stay in Andalusia in an unusually diplomatic manner.

'Have you reached any decision about the post I offered to you, Señorita Ross? Studying the eagles' habits and habitat could develop into a lonely and exhausting chore if it were to be allowed to absorb the whole of your attention. So, as you so obviously love the company of children, don't you think that a few hours spent teaching might help to break up the monotony of your day?'

The tone of sweet reasonableness fell strangely from the lips of the Conde with the aloof, inscrutable expression and proud dark head, silvered at each temple with the markings of the Spanish imperial eagle. Yet even though she felt suspicious of his change of tactics, she could not refute the logic of his statement.

Made nervous by a watchful, heavily-pressing silence, she gave a short, breathless laugh before chirping with artificial brightness:

'You win, Conde! Very well, I'll do as you ask, but on one condition—please try to persuade Sabelita that she's mistaken in her assumption that you brought me to Andalusia with the purpose of making me your bride!'

She had expected him to respond with amusement to her quip, was even prepared—because he was so unpredictable and because he so rarely smiled—to have her jocundity deflated with a frown, but the reaction that clamped down upon his features the tightness of pain, his air of offended pride and piercing glance of displeasure, made her feel instantly rebuked, threatened as a cowering concubine.

'You disappoint me, *señorita*,' he iced, rising to his feet so that he appeared to tower tall as the high sierras. 'One thing I had not thought it necessary to warn you against was the indiscretion of gossiping with servants! Sabelita shall be reprimanded for her impertinence and for disobeying an order—an order which I now pass on to you and which you would do well to act upon. *The subject of my marriage is taboo!*' he stressed with a bitterness that struck her as appalling. 'Once, as is well known to all in Andalusia, I was on the verge of marrying a girl whom I had known and loved since childhood. Two days before the ceremony was due to take place the marriage was cancelled, with no reason given other than that Maria had had a change of heart and mind. Her father, however, made no secret of that fact that it was he who had brought pressure to bear upon his only child, he who had striven hard to convince her that one drop of gypsy blood instilled deceit, cruelty and a nomadic wanderlust into a man's veins! Since then, *señorita*, I have remained betrothed to the state of bachelordom—as good is betrothed to evil, as life is betrothed to death, as Andalusian families are betrothed to the religion of unadulterated blood and impeccable breeding!' He spun aside, crushing a herb plant underfoot so that the scent of the flower of love eddied in the air and hung potent and powerfully overwhelming. 'Is your curiosity now satisfied, *señorita*?' Judging her horrified silence as an affirmative, he iced conclusively, 'Good! If ever in future you should consider yourself entitled to pry further into my private affairs, I should be obliged if you would approach *me* with your questions, and not my garrulous servants!'

CHAPTER SIX

'*Uno ... dos ... tres ... quatro ... cinco ... seis ... siete ... ocho ... nueve ... diez!*'

Frances beamed approval upon her class of urchin pupils, who had responded with enthusiasm to her request to be assured that they really had memorised the first ten cardinal numbers.

'*Muy bonita!*' she applauded, pretending not to notice the two boys who were sidling out of their seats with the obvious intention of making a getaway, or the writhing bulge underneath the pinafore of a little girl who could not bear to be parted from a kitten whose muffled, indignant mews had accompanied the entire lesson.

The Conde had been right in his assumption that gypsy children would respond better to coaxing than to coercion. Each day since the school had opened the previous week, chairs and tables had been ranged in front of a blackboard and easel set beneath the shade of a tree for the benefit of the pale young *maestra* who had come from England, a land they had heard had a climate as cold and inhospitable as the peaks of the Sierra Nevada which for six months of the year remained covered in snow.

For the first couple of days Frances had been disheartened by the lack of response from children who had laughed, played, and cavorted at a distance near enough to monitor her movements

yet far enough away to maintain a safe distance
between themselves and the *maestra* who represented a threat to their freedom. Then gradually,
shyly, one by one, the seats had become filled.
More had been added and still more, until a
situation had been reached where, having had to
intervene in fights arising from disputed claims to
territory, she had finally persuaded the latest
arrivals each to fetch a chair from home.

The freezing formality of the Conde towards his
guest at dinner each evening had softened with
each good report he had received of her progress,
so much so that she had been surprised and
disconcerted when, the previous evening, after she
had refused dessert and politely requested leave to
retire to her room, he had waved her back into her
chair and pushed within reach a dish of shelled
almonds.

'Try one, you'll find them very good,' he had
encouraged, setting an example by splitting a crisp
kernel between white teeth. 'Now, I'd like to know
what impressions you have formed about your
pupils, their homes and their parents. But first of
all, I must ask your permission to dispense with
the obligation of having to use a form of address
that renders conversation stilted and consequently
more difficult. If you have no objection, I would
prefer you to call me Romanes, which after all,' he
had shrugged, 'is merely the gypsy word for
"man". May I, in return, be permitted to address
you as Frances?'

She had responded with the blush of a fiery
peony and signified agreement with a nod of her
head, relieved by this evidence of his lessening

displeasure, yet fully aware that she would never feel sufficiently relaxed in his company to allow the intimate name to falter from her lips . . .

'All right, children, you may go now!' She clapped her hands to signal dismissal. 'Lessons will be resumed at four o'clock, if you'd care to join me. We could make a start upon translating into Spanish some of your favourite songs and rhymes.'

She was gathering up her books, wilting a little in spite of the canopy of leaves shading her from the worst of the noonday sun, when a different male voice attracted her attention.

'Permiso, señorita!'

She spun round to direct a look of smiling enquiry towards Culvato, father of the child who was inseparable from her kitten.

'. . . Floure, my wife, has sent me to ask whether,' he paused to clear his throat then, appearing shyly embarrassed, concluded in a hurried rush of words, 'you would honour us by sharing our meal?'

Feeling flattered yet undecided, Frances glanced towards the road. Sometimes the Conde arrived in his car to drive her back to the Palacio for lunch, at other times he sent a servant, but today her transport was almost an hour overdue and the only sign of movement to be seen on the road cutting straight through the ravine where the gypsies' caves were situated was a shimmering heat haze.

The temptation to learn more about this race of people whose innate sense of gaiety was conveyed in the richness of multi-coloured skirts worn by its barefooted, hip-swinging womenfolk, and by the coins used as buttons, the golden earrings and colourfully braided waistcoats of its men, proved irresistible. Also, there was the bonus of being allowed to make a closer inspection of their very unusual homes.

'Thank you, Culvato,' she smiled acceptance to the man who had been introduced to her by the Conde as the leader of the tribe, 'I'm grateful to you and to your wife, Floure, for your kindness and will gladly accept your invitation.'

Because of a combination of circumstances—the fact that the Conde's simmering annoyance had led him to provide the basic essentials for an open-air schoolroom and no more; because of her own innate shyness, and because of uncertainty on the part of the gypsies in whose midst she had been dumped whether to welcome her with a show of friendship or to treat her with deferential awe—she had been made to feel as if she was neither fish, flesh, fowl nor good red herring, the recipient of many encouraging grins and nods yet left stranded within a chair-littered clearing affording tantalising glimpses of caves gouged out of hills of clay, a honeycomb of homes housing a swarm of gypsies buzzing through one door and out of another with the fervour of busy bees.

'Then if you would step this way, señorita,' Culvato beamed, addressing her slowly in Spanish that had a distinctly different dialect which, during the past week, she had become gradually able to decipher, except for gaps left in sentences by the occasional use of gypsy jargon.

Eagerly she accompanied him towards the hive of stone-faced homes emitting smoke from small, rounded chimneys, their whitewashed walls festooned with strings of bright red peppers and hanging baskets spilling a profusion of pink, white and red geraniums. Huge earthenware pots crammed with herbs lined an exquisitely scented path towards each door, and smaller pots held in place with a thin circle of wire beneath each rim were positioned so that a stream of cool green ivy seemed to flow downwards from the roofs, around arched doorways, and unglazed black-grilled windows.

Floure, accompanied by Cinerella, her youngest child, was waiting in the doorway, her brown face split by a happy, white-toothed smile of welcome.

'*Droboy tune romale, señorita!*' She bobbed a curtsey and motioned to her daughter to do the same.

'*Nais tuke!*' Frances faltered, parodying as exactly as she was able Sabelita's words of response to the traditional Romany greeting.

Her effort was rewarded with cries of delight, and as she responded to the family's smiles the impression Frances received was one of happiness, health and vitality. Floure was looking especially vivacious, her ample curves draped in a low-cut, many-layered, ankle-length dress the colour of poppy petals clustered around a shiny head of blue-black hair, braided so as to form a frame for large expressive eyes, strong white teeth, and thickly stroked eyebrows and lashes. Both she and Culvato were wearing jewellery fashioned from ancient coins—necklaces and bracelets for Floure, and for Culvato earrings that hung low as the magenta silk kerchief wound around his neck, and a medallion exposed by a buttonless shirt divided across the dark matt skin of his bared chest. Neither mother nor daughter was wearing shoes, and as they preceded her into the cave dwelling Frances was struck by their pride of bearing and lissom, graceful walk.

But immediately she stepped past a thick wooden door hung with ancient iron bolts she was entranced by the sight of rough interior walls contrasting dazzling white against a red-flagstoned floor; burnished copper pans and kettles, an assortment of cheap but colourful ornaments, painted wooden chairs with woven rush seats, and a large open-hooded fireplace, empty of fuel, except for a small square portion in one corner of the hearth where fir-cones had been tossed on to red hot embers to provide just sufficient heat to keep the contents of a large stewpot simmering. Half hidden behind the shimmer of beaded curtains Frances glimpsed two smaller rooms furnished with brass bedsteads and brilliantly striped quilts to match handwoven rugs scattered at random over a cool flagged floor.

As she smiled acceptance of the seat Culvato had hastily positioned where it would catch the maximum amount of breeze from the open doorway, Cinerella stooped to pick a deep red carnation from a pitcherful set in a shady corner and began shyly advancing towards her with the clove-scented gift.

'*Gracias*, Cinerella,' she accepted, charmed by the simple gesture of friendship offered by a child whose solemn expression was belied by twinkling, mischievous eyes.

A table had already been set with two rows of blue and white dishes the size of soup plates, and immediately Floure began dishing out stew from the simmering pot a horde of hungry-looking urchins appeared as if from nowhere and began jostling for position at the table. Casting Frances a quick look of apology, Floure served them first, then shooed them with their plates of stew and hunks of bread to sit lining the walls before drawing three chairs up to the table.

'Will you sit here, *señorita*?' She indicated a place set to the left of Culvato, who was waiting to take his seat at the head of the table. The thick, delicious stew was lightly spiced and barely salted, but the taste of fowl and game was enhanced by the flavour of herbs, especially wild garlic, and by the berries, mushrooms and nettles that formed the basis of the surprisingly tasty vegetable content.

Interpreting anxiety in Floure's watchful look, Frances slowly savoured her first mouthful, then, conscious of the entire household's breath-held attention, did not hesitate to convey her appreciation.

'Mmm ... delicious!' she murmured, emphasising her enjoyment by scooping up a second spoonful. 'I don't think I've ever tasted a more flavourful concoction!'

As if her words were the signal they had all been waiting for, the silence was broken by an outburst of chattering from the children, Floure's relieved laughter, and a vote of thanks from her smiling husband.

'Everyone agrees that my wife is a wonderful

cook, *señorita*, I told her that she had no cause to worry, that you were certain to enjoy your meal.'

'Which could only be as good as the produce you supplied,' Floure reminded him fondly, obviously well pleased. 'My man is an expert provider,' she boasted proudly, 'which is just as well considering the number of mouths he has to feed.'

With an audacious twinkle lighting his dark eyes, Culvato confided to Frances, 'We gypsies have always been a race of gatherers and collectors. Being neither hunters nor farmers, we have learnt to feed well from nature—berries, mushrooms, roots, wild fruits, fish and all things furred and feathered are supplied in abundance by the Creator. The fruits of the earth belong to all men. Game and fowl are there for the taking, only the eating of dog, cat, or horse flesh is strictly taboo. Did you know, *señorita*,' mercifully, he had not seemed to notice her fastidious wince, 'that it was we gypsies who first invented artificial baits for line fishing and also the artificial fly for tempting trout? We are also expert at making bait with gum obtained from plants, and with certain types of oil which when smeared on to stones has an attraction so potent that fish swarm towards it. Non-gypsies who witnessed such a sight have even been heard to swear that the shoals have been magicked!'

Warming to his theme, he leant forward to confide, 'The art of baiting a trap and rigging a snare was taught to me, and to my brother Rom, by my late father. Rom, as chief patron of our tribe, and myself being the eldest son of its leader, were expected to be expert at all gypsy rites and rituals long before other boys of the same age.'

Wearing the faintest of frowns, Floure interrupted her husband's flow of words.

'Culvato means no disrespect when he refers to El Conde as his brother, you understand, *señorita*. Though a nobleman by birth, he is regarded as one of us—as a member of our family.'

'Disrespect!' Culvato rose to his feet, obviously incensed. 'Are you *loca*, woman?' he snorted, making his meaning plain by employing the derisive gesture of screwing a finger-knuckle hard against his temple. 'Why should you find it necessary to explain any of the words that I use in connection with my brother? Does not Rom share our camp and our food as only a brother is permitted to do? Has he not sworn the gypsy oath while touching my chest with the tip of his knife, and was he not christened with a gypsy name while his wrists were bound together with gold-coloured ribbon? *Of course he is my brother!'* he exploded, wrath spilling into his eyes with the turbulence of a racing torrent. 'To whom did he come for comfort after being jilted by his faithless *novia*? And who else but myself did he choose to accompany him on the bout of wild revelry with which he finally managed to rout the devil of desire from his aching loins?'

'Bah!' Floure's meaning would have been clear in any language, even without the added enlightenment provided by a curled-up lip and a contemptuous flick of her fingers. 'For years you have used Rom's disappointment in love as an excuse for absenting yourselves for weeks whenever either of

you felt the need for a space of freedom! Why
can't you simply admit that such trips are
necessary in order to assuage the nomadic urge to
wander that fires every gypsy's veins?' she accused,
dark eyes flashing. 'I too feel the ties of family
growing irksome; I too am gypsy,' she stabbed a
pointing finger among coins dangling like a golden
collar around her neck, then almost spat at her
startled husband. 'As well as being united in
marriage, I also share your love of freedom, your
need to escape from the bonds imposed by the
duty to nurture our children, yet what rage would
erupt inside you if *I* were to give in to the desire to
be my own mistress, if I were to show contempt
for the consequences and disappear for weeks to
live in accordance with nature's rhythm! Go with
your brother if you must,' Floure stamped her
foot, obviously working herself up to a point
where years of simmering resentment was to be
allowed to boil over, 'but be honest about your
motives, *both of you*! Rom was never truly in love
with Maria Peralta! To him, she was merely a
childhood companion who never grew up, a
playful kitten who never matured into the sort of
passionate female necessary to captivate, tantalise
and respond with abandon to his needs. What sort
of woman,' she scoffed angrily, smoothing com-
placent hands over ample hips, 'would allow
herself to be talked out of marriage to the man she
loved by a doting father who feared a lonely old
age? When Maria Peralta jilted the most eligible
bachelor in the whole of Andalusia, using an
excuse provided by her bull-breeding father that
the family bloodstock had to be kept pure, not

only did she outrage members of her own society,
she also condemned herself to a lifetime as a
spinster, because all other men have been scared
off, afraid that they might not measure up to her
exacting standards! But justice has been done!
While she has been left like an ornament to gather
dust upon a shelf, every other girl in Andalusia
has been plainly eager to console Rom for his
imaginary disappointment! Huh!' her shoulders
heaved in a contemptuous shrug, 'his lucky
deliverance, more like!'

'*Woman!*' Culvato found his voice, 'you talk too
much!' Thumping his fist hard down upon the
table, he accused, 'Have you forgotten that we
have a guest in our house, and also,' he swept an
arm towards his gawping children, 'that we now
have a row of little pitchers filled with gossip up to
their brims?' Angrily, he dispersed his curious
brood. '*Anda! Anda!*' he cried out, loudly clapping
his hands.

As if the slap that resulted had served as a
reminder of some previous punishment, the
children leapt to their feet and ran, leaving behind
a floor littered with licked-clean plates.

Feeling completely stunned, looking dazed as a
tourist who has wandered by accident into the
midst of a volcanic eruption, Frances sat rooted,
staring at the two antagonists glaring fury at each
other across the width of the table. Never in her
life before had she witnessed such a show of fiery
temperament, heard words rippling like a knife
through flesh, seen glances gouging deep as an
angry wound, felt seared by a passion as
tempestuous in anger as it no doubt was in love.

Shaking with reaction, she rose to her feet with the intention of creeping as silently as possible away from the arena of wrath where any moment, she felt convinced, Floure might whip a dagger out of a garter hugging a shapely thigh, or Culvato might begin meaningfully unbuckling the clasp of his broad leather belt.

But at the sound of her chair scraping across the flagstones, two pairs of dark eyes unlocked and swung in her direction. Visibly she shrank, feeling the panic of a rabbit about to be used as a scapegoat by a couple of snarling whippets, then almost collapsed with relief when she saw savage glares become submerged by waves of compassion.

At the sight of her distressed face Culvato struck the palm of his hand against his forehead. '*A thousand pardons!* Floure,' he spun quickly towards his troubled wife, 'fetch water, you've almost frightened the life out of the *pobre Inglesa* with your display of insane jealousy!'

In spite of the monstrously unjust accusation, Floure did not stop to argue but hurried to fetch a pitcherful of sweet spring water.

'Drink up, *maestra*,' she urged, pushing an earthenware mug into Frances' nerveless hands, then as she watched her drink she stepped back to remark with an inscrutable smile, 'A man in a passion rides a runaway horse, but you were never in any danger of being trampled, *señorita*. Grievances are best squeezed like sour pips from the sweet heart of an orange, so that nothing remains to stick in the throat. What you have just witnessed was no more than a bout of harmless badinage—beware of passions that are silent,' she nodded sagely. 'In nature, it is the mute, silently creeping snake that is responsible for the most tragic acts of violence!'

'Merely the mention of such a reptile in her hearing will be sufficient to instil fear of a wriggling piece of string into the heart of the timid *maestra*!'

Frances almost dropped her mug when a dry observation was directed from the open doorway.

'I must apologise for arriving late,' the Conde sauntered inside the cave, 'but it appears that I was right to console my conscience with the assurance that Floure and Culvato would not permit you to starve.' His glance swept over the table laden with discarded dishes, the depleted stewpot, and lingered upon a bowlful of pomegranates and figs that had remained untouched. 'I take it that you have finished eating, Frances?' he enquired, addressing her by name without the least trace of unease. 'If not, please carry on, I'll wait outside until you have finished.'

'Rom, old friend!' Culvato exclaimed, striding forward to clasp his hands around his. 'What are you implying—that there is no room for my brother in my home, or that to grace such a hovel as this with his presence is beneath my brother's dignity?'

'Neither,' the Conde smiled, returning Culvato's handshake with a warmth that showed confidence that no serious rebuke had been intended. 'I did not come alone, therefore courtesy demands that if there is to be a delay I must wait outside and keep my friend company.'

Galvanised into action by the threat of being

cast once more into a maelstrom of unpredictable
gypsy temperament, Frances assured him hur-
riedly,

'I couldn't eat another bite.' Then mindful of
her manners, she turned to her smiling host and
hostess. 'I enjoyed my meal so much, thank you
for inviting me.'

'Your presence at our table has given us both
great pleasure, *señorita*,' Floure responded with an
aplomb that convinced Frances that the row she
had just witnessed was as of little consequence to
the volatile-natured couple as a dead leaf cast from
nowhere on a hot breath of wind.

'Soon, at a time that is convenient to yourself
and to our brother Rom, we must arrange a
proper visit. We'll have a *fiesta*!' Floure decided,
clasping her hands together like an excited child.
'A gathering lasting all night long, during which
all the family will entertain in turn, terminating
with our grandmother, who can truly be termed
the matriarch of old-style flamenco. Listening to
her songs, *señorita*, will help you to understand
how much music means to us gypsies, how it
makes us feel good and helps us to forget the
sorrows that are deep inside of us. Promise me
that you will come,' she urged, then swung
pleading eyes towards the Conde. 'Please, Rom,
say that you will bring the young *maestra* to our
fiesta?'

After hesitating for a fraction of a second, he
shrugged, then conceded kindly,

'As you say, Floure, the mixture of the Moorish,
the Andalusian and the gypsy contained within
flamenco should provide insight into a life that is

full of contradictions. It is only fair that one who has offered to instruct our children should not remain ignorant of the most intimate and ancient ways of gypsy living.'

Vaguely, it had impinged upon Frances's conscience that the Conde, looking lithe, tall and straight, dressed all in black, with a tight, waist-length jacket and black Cordoban hat, was dressed for riding, nevertheless she was not prepared for the encounter that took place immediately she stepped outside the cave dwelling.

Two beautiful Arab horses with arrogantly tossing heads were pawing the ground, a black stallion that was riderless, and a snow-white mare bearing an elegant, stiff-backed rider in the saddle. A girl, alone, beautifully turned out in a long black riding skirt, a short, severely-tailored jacket made to appear deliciously feminine with the addition of a white silk stock worn high at the neck, and with a wide black sombrero casting a pool of shadow across patrician features set pale and cool as a cameo.

At the sight of his companion, Floure and Culvato stepped hastily backward, as if anxious to seek anonymity within the solitude of their home, leaving Frances to flounder alone in a sea of embarrassment while the girl's calculating eyes assessed every wayward wisp of hair, every smudge of chalk dust on the limp shirt and crumpled denims worn by the girl for whom she had been kept waiting.

'*Cara,*' even as the Conde spoke Frances guessed the identity of the girl whom he was about to introduce, 'I'd like you to make the acquaint-

ance of Señorita Frances Ross, the young *maestra*
who is coping so well with her class of unruly
pupils. Frances,' he glinted down at her, a slight
twitching of his lips convincing her that he was
enjoying her hot, sticky discomfiture, 'permit me
to introduce a very old friend, Señorita Maria
Peralta, daughter of my nearest neighbour,
Gonzales, Carlos Peralta, Marqués de Quesada!'

CHAPTER SEVEN

MARIA'S eyes, when she glanced at the Conde across the width of a wrought iron table set out on the patio, were the soft, velvet brown of pansies. Yet, except where he was concerned, she appeared formidably aloof, especially towards Frances who, in a freshly laundered blouse and well worn skirt, was feeling humble as dust beneath the dainty feet of the girl whose appearance had caused Sabelita to mutter darkly,

'A beautiful face and wicked mind, often, full often, together we find!'

'Do you intend staying long in Andalusia, Señorita Ross?' Maria enquired coolly.

Carefully, Frances laid down the knife with which she had been attempting to peel a peach and slid trembling hands beneath the table, clenching her fingers hard together until the knuckles showed white as she fought to regain the composure that had fled the moment the Conde had leant sideways in his saddle, plucked her from the ground, and held her firmly in front of him as he had urged the black Arab stallion into an easy canter.

The journey home had been a nightmare, a frenzied furore of blushing, tingling, quivering, throbbing agitation which, because of Maria's close attention, had had to be endured with a show of stony indifference. Some instinct had told her that the entire incident had been planned, that the intimate trap—with herself as the victim and Maria as the furious onlooker—had been deliberately sprung by the man who could be as cruel in his own way as the Moor whose streak of sadistic humour had led him to use his enemies' skulls as decorative flower pots.

'Well?' Maria prompted, made impatient by Frances' look of dazed hesitation. 'Is your visit to last a week, a month, or perhaps just a few more days?'

'Frances will be remaining with us for an indefinite period.' Smoothly, the Conde came to her rescue, not merely with a reply to her questioner, but also by reaching for the plate holding the discarded peach which he competently stripped of its skin before pushing it back towards Frances with the confusing comment, 'Sometimes, I find myself regretting the passing of the era of the powerful caliphs whose wishes were considered law and thereby granted with the swiftness of a command. They would have had no need to cajole and coax, to be forever racking their brains in an effort to think of some inducement that might persuade a *maestra* to remain permanently in Andalusia.'

'Why should *you* wish to do that?' Maria's gasped intake of breath, the dagger-swift sharpness of her response, sounded plainly to Frances like a reaction of fear, fear of being usurped, of being deprived of the power she undoubtedly still held over the emotions of the man whose rejection as a husband she was obviously bitterly regretting.

'Surely my reason is obvious?' Puzzled by the

tender, meaningful cadences in his voice, Frances abandoned her study of the neatly dissected peach and glanced upwards, then blushed to the roots of her hair when she saw his deeply intimate look trained upon her face, his pensive half-smile, and the sombre clouding of his features which anyone less knowledgeable than herself might easily have mistaken for an expression of intense longing.

Her glance fell upon Maria, sitting still as a frozen mute, sympathising with her pain when, like a man whose revenge-fevered blood can only be cured by the letting of the blood of another, the Conde intensified her misery with the warm attribution,

'Frances' method of handling wayward pupils has proved so successful that we are reluctant to even acknowledge the possibility of her departure.'

Frances' feeling of pity was ousted by annoyance when with a malicious snap of her perfect teeth Maria returned the spiteful rejoinder,

'I had imagined that ill-disciplined, ill-mannered gypsy children would be more in need of a mature person specially trained to deal with the offspring of parents who seem incapable of inhibiting their own unruly tempers, their idle disinclination to work, their instinct to steal whatever food they fancy and to respond to justifiable protests with expressions that are often rude and mostly unintelligible. Children need firm discipline, Rom, and quite frankly, *querido*, your English Miss appears to me to be far too immature to exert authority or to administer severe punishment.'

Frances sensed the Conde's narrow-eyed search for her reaction, saw him relax in his chair with a cheroot clenched between his teeth, smiling in the manner of a potentate preparing to enjoy some scene about to be played out especially for his amusement—but she was far too incensed to care!

'Certainly children need to be disciplined, Señorita Peralta,' she agreed coldly, 'but it is possible to instil decent standards of behaviour, to give clear guidance of what is right and what is wrong, of what kind of behaviour is acceptable and what kind is not, without having to resort to tyranny. Failure to teach pupils the elementary laws of life is a betrayal of the teacher's primary function. A product of my own experience is the belief that there are no really wicked children— only imitators of lazy or misguided adults!'

'*Your* experience!' Maria's trill of scornful laughter sent flags of colour flying high in Frances' cheeks. 'And when, might one ask, did you gain such a huge amount of experience?' she jeered. 'During the few years you spent at college, perhaps?'

'Partly,' Frances stated simply, 'but mostly during the many happy years I spent as a child myself.'

When a stunned silence fell over the occupants of the table set in a patio made shady by an overhead trellis woven with tendrils of leafy greenery, fragrant with the scent of flowers spilling in colourful profusion from decorative tubs, made tranquil by the musical sound of water playing faintly in the background, Frances felt no triumph at a loss of composure that had left Maria speechless, floundering for words to begin a counter-attack against defeat that had been accomplished by a few quietly spoken words of logic.

The Conde's choked-back growl of laughter aggravated rather than helped to defuse the situation, and though his expression was quickly rendered unreadable, the hint of a quirk playing around his lips indicated to Frances, at least, that he had found the contest of wills entertaining.

Perhaps it was this hint of enjoyment that alerted Maria's sensitive Andalusian pride, because in spite of eyes flashing a look of dedicated enmity, a slim frame stiff with the leashed fury of a cat tempted to spring, she managed a shrug that dismissed the subject as being of little consequence and evoked Frances' unwilling admiration by issuing a carefully modulated invitation.

'If your visit is to be prolonged until Easter, Señorita Ross, you must join our party for the week-long *feria*, a time during which Andalusia becomes a playground offering bullfights, displays of superb horsemanship, flamenco music, carnivals and parades enhanced by females of all ages wearing our colourful, eye-catching traditional dress. However,' she rose to her feet, managing to transmit an impression of having tolerated for too long a conversation she found boring, 'a word of warning should not come amiss.' Momentarily, her eyes flickered towards the Conde, who was politely rising to his feet. 'This is the region of the notorious Don Juan, the shameless libertine whose exploits are still being copied by many present-day rakes. During the *feria*, according to legend, even the devil has the permission of God to tempt . . .'

Good manners dictated that Frances should

accompany Maria and the Conde to the stables where their mounts had been left in the care of grooms prior to their departure. So with burning cheeks and an air of discomfiture enveloping her like a contemptuously flung cloak, she trailed in Maria's shadow, suffering her malicious glances and supposed overtures of friendship.

'We must arrange a date when it will be convenient for you to visit my home, Señorita Ross.' Small, perfect teeth bared in a smile of condescension. 'My father is always eager to show off his herd of fighting bulls that is the result of hundreds of years of careful breeding aimed at producing the characteristics most desirable in the bullring—supreme courage, strength, and stamina. Some claim that the Andalusian-bred bull is the most dangerous animal in the world. Certainly, whenever a bull has been put inside a cage with a lion or a tiger, the bull has always survived the experiment. Even the elephant, though protected from mortal injury by his thick hide, has been known to attempt an escape, totally terrorised. Our ranch covers many thousand of acres of harsh land where the grazing is thin but extremely nourishing. Bull calves are born in winter and left to roam free, to forage where they can, to fight whenever they want to, consequently those that manage to survive the winter provide proof of their strength and durability.'

'And what happens to those that don't?' Frances' voice was husky with compassion.

Maria shrugged. 'Any animal that does not achieve the required standard of bravery is either raised for beef or disposed of immediately.

Breeders cannot afford to be sentimental, bullfighting is an art form, an expression of Andaluz
temperament which combines an eye for graceful
movement, admiration of courage, lust for excitement, with proud hauteur and just a hint of
barbarity.'

Frances shuddered, resisting an impulse to
follow the direction of Maria's glance that had
homed like a pigeon towards the silent man
sauntering by their side, adjusting his rangy stride
to the tip-tapping progress of high-heeled riding
boots and the reluctant drag of cork-soled sandals.
Sickened by the thought of animals being bred
solely for the purpose of slaughter, she protested,

'How can you possibly find pleasure in killing
for killing's sake? Have you no feeling of pity for
the unfortunate bull who is given no choice but to
star in the savage pastime you term entertainment!'

Maria's look of scorn was as predictable as the
Conde's cold query.

'Unfortunate?' he swung round to condemn. 'I
think not! When the time arrives for the bull to
fight his last fight he has enjoyed five wild,
glorious years of freedom on the range. Wouldn't
any creature, given a choice, turn down the
sluggish existence of a steer condemned to chewing
his way nearer and nearer extinction inside a
slaughterhouse in favour of the honour of being
chosen to star in the *lidia*, a pageant with a history
that can be traced back almost five thousand years
from the times of the Cretans, the Greeks and
Phoenicians, right through to the Arab occupation
of Spain? Even Spanish conquistadors tried out

their lance work on the highly combative animals in order to maintain form for fighting in battle. I cannot argue with your view that bullfighting is not a sport, for the outcome is predictable, therefore there is no contest. But neither is it the type of gory spectacle relished by Englishmen who follow packs of hounds in pursuit of small red foxes merely to claim as a prize the bloody brush that is all that remains after the dogs have caught and worried their prey. By comparison, the ritual of the bullfight is an art form, a dramatic pageant that portrays the ability of both man and beast to show dignity and courage while dicing with death!'

As she sat high in the saddle, displaying the proud, straight-backed carriage for which Andalusian riders are famed, probably nothing could have been more calculated to restore Maria's good humour than the sight of her verbal antagonist standing with head bowed, scuffling the soles of her sandals in the dust, as she waited to wave farewell to their guest and her sharply-spoken champion.

When an elongated shadow fell across the ground at her feet, Frances sighed and raised a pale, chastened face towards the Conde, expecting further rebuke, then she stared wide-eyed with wonder when she saw that he was smiling. Across his shoulder she caught a glimpse of Maria's hardening expression before earth, sky and landscape were blotted out when deliberately he lowered his head until his firm, rather cruel mouth was resting lightly as a bee drawing nectar from sweetly-parted lips, quivering soft and pink as flower petals.

'I shall return as quickly as I can, *querida*,' his husky promise was pitched just loud enough for Maria to overhear. 'I suggest that you rest in the coolness of your room.' With a show of concern that appeared incredibly genuine he stroked a tendril of hair back from her brow and scolded tenderly, 'Pale English flowers tend to wilt beneath the blazing Andalusian sun—I shall expect to see your fresh young beauty completely restored when you join me for dinner this evening.'

Rendered dumb and incapable of movement, Frances watched dazedly as the high-stepping thoroughbreds carried their riders into the lush Andalusian *vega*.

'Why . . .?' she breathed, concentrating her mind upon the riders receding swiftly into the distance, not daring even to begin analysing strange emotions that had been stirred into life by the tight clasp of his arms holding her safely in the saddle and which ever since had responded with a wince or a throb to every scathing word, every casual look exchanged up until their last breathtaking encounter. 'Why does he find it necessary to use me as a barrier between himself and Maria when they are such a perfectly matched pair, as right together as night is with day, bitter with sweet, as a sin-black stallion is with a virginal white mare?'

Long after horses and riders had disappeared out of sight she remained staring into space, then, becoming conscious of the heat of the sun on her bared head and a throbbing at each temple, she turned on her heel to seek relief inside the cool interior of the Palacio. As usual, whenever she set foot inside the majestic marbled hall with its high-domed ceiling, portraits, heirlooms, and a smell of antiquity that reminded her of cathedrals, she experienced the awe of an impoverished interloper confronted with trappings of wealth undreamt of, a weight of great fortune that imposed bonds as heavy as those of slavery.

She was lost in thought, staring fixedly at a porcelain plate beautifully decorated with gold leaf and bearing a painting on its base of a pair of Oriental golden pheasants, the cock proudly strutting, flaunting his colourful plumage before a cooing, adoring hen, when a sibilant voice hissed past her shoulder,

'The tail feathers of a strutting cock bring luck in the search for love!' Sabelita nodded, indicating the plate with the painted tableau. 'Girls must resort to magic if their love affairs go awry. If you wish it, *señorita*, I could concoct for you a love potion which, when administered secretly in a drink, will turn the coldest-hearted man into a passionate lover. My potions *always* work,' she promised, 'provided the one who administers them is good and pure in love. Tell me the date of your birth,' she urged eagerly, 'down to the exact minute, so that I may know exactly which stones, flowers, herbs and oils to gather, as well as the exact time to mix the potion in order to ensure maximum strength?'

With a blush that gave immediate lie to her words, Frances stammered a hasty refusal.

'Don't be foolish, Sabelita! What need have I of a love potion? And as for El Conde, I should

imagine he would be the last man in the world to
need help with his love affairs.'

'Love is necessary to all who wish to live life as
it ought to be lived,' Sabelita insisted fiercely,
'happily, and with many nights of glorious
passion! Provided that you are truly in love, and
that the man in your life is not in love with
another, a few sips of my magic philtre will
transport you both to the gates of paradise.'

Deciding that the embarrassing conversation
had gone on long enough, Frances attempted a
humorous side-step away from the subject.

'If I were to arrive there this minute, I doubt
whether I would be allowed in,' she quipped,
glancing ruefully at the skirt that was growing
shabbier with every passing day.

When Sabelita glared and tossed her dark head
until hooped golden earrings jangled, Frances
stepped back in haste, reminded of tales she had
heard about the gypsies' witch-like ability to cast
spells, for good and evil, as well as their reputed
gift for foretelling the future.

'You poke fun at me, *señorita*,' the old woman
almost spat, 'which means that I am now forced to
prove beyond doubt that my potions, collected by
many generations of my family who travelled the
world learning the secrets of old alchemists and
sorcerers of the East, really *do* work!'

When she flounced off in a huff, Frances
frowned and bite worriedly into her bottom lip.
Then heaving a sigh of resignation she walked
towards the stairs, feeling tossed and battered by
emotion, yearning for the peaceful atmosphere of
her bedroom where, with the key turned in the

lock, she could feel protected, at least physically, from the aggravating, exasperating, overpowering inhabitants of the Palacio del Flamenco.

In spite of a built-in resistance to following advice given like a command, the divan with its shimmering blue cover and silken sheets drew her as if magnetised and fulfilled its promise of bliss immediately she laid her aching head upon a soft cloud of pillows. Determined to stay awake, to mull over her thoughts, to drag her heart from a morass of confused emotions, she fixed her gaze directly ahead, intending to clear her mind by concentrating for a while upon a portion of the pale, carved wooden panelling lining the walls of the room.

At the first she had no difficulty identifying crescent moons, ears of wheat, the horseshoes, horns and stars that were typical Eastern emblems of good luck and fertility. But gradually, the fur and feather, beaks, claws and teeth of birds and animals began blurring behind a screen of wavering lashes, then finally vanished as she sank into a deep sleep.

The room was full of shadows when, some hours later, her slumber was disturbed by a slight sound that sent her lashes flying upwards over her drowsy eyes. Lazily she stirred, then while lifting a hand to smother a yawn she stiffened, wide eyes questioning the movement of a patch of dark shadow lowering towards the bed.

'Don't be alarmed, *cara*,' a familiar voice soothed. 'I merely came to remind you that it is almost time to dress for dinner.'

'I don't possess a dress, as you must surely have noticed, *señor*!' The shocked puzzlement in her

voice was reflected in accusing grey eyes. 'Are you
in the habit of entering a lady's bedroom without
asking permission? If so, I must remember in
future to lock——'

She lapsed into sudden silence. She *had* locked
her door!

With a gesture of mockery, he drew aside to
indicate a hollow gap in the length of wall
panelling.

'Behind there lies a secret passageway connecting
this room with my own,' he smiled, bending nearer
so that an eagle-fierce head with silver-tipped
wings seemed to swoop towards her out of the
darkness, 'an indication, I suppose, that promi-
scuity must not be considered a prerogative of the
present century,' he concluded, displaying an ease
of manner which for some inexplicable reason left
her feeling intensely affronted.

Striving hard to hide her fear of the man whose
moods ran the gamut of Spanish hauteur, Romany
passion and Moorish arrogance, she stormed at his
shadowy outline.

'Whatever vices there are in the world, *Conde*, I
feel certain that an ancestor of yours must have
been in on their inception! The tree of sin spreads
roots that strike deeper with each passing decade,
throwing up shoots that develop in its own
likeness!'

'Just as I, too, am certain,' he responded in a
tone silken as the stroke of his hand along the
tender curve of her neck, 'that females who make a
vice out of virtue are often driven into doing so by
lack of temptation. However,' he turned swiftly
aside, 'I came here not to rob you of your virtue,

but to attempt to preserve it. Maria, prompted by the most charitable of motives, has drawn my attention to the fact that your presence un-chaperoned in my home could give rise to unpleasant speculation. I have therefore decided,' he informed her coolly, 'that as tradition has imposed upon me the duty to produce an heir, the solution to both our problems can be provided by a simple contract of marriage.'

Frances wanted to move, to fling herself off the bed and run as far away as possible from the calculating, emotionless devil who regarded mar-riage merely as a solution to a problem. But the touch of his fingers against the virginal skin of a neck that had never before felt the power of a man's caress had rendered her body weak, flame-devoured, and utterly boneless.

'Well . . .?' His threatening shadow wheeled, then loomed towards her. 'Have you no answer to my proposal?'

'Is that what it was?' she managed to force through a throat so tight she could barely swallow. 'I thought you were offering me a contract, a merger of two bodies with the object of ensuring continuity of an established institution.'

She could not see his face, yet she sensed from his immediate stillness that his expression was wary.

'You find such an idea distasteful?' The words hissed from his lips as he bent towards her. Then without giving her time to draw breath he pounced, plucking her from her nest of pillows into arms that lashed her body hard against his tautly-muscled chest.

'How remiss of me to have overlooked the possiblity of a child betraying a tendency towards womanhood once in a while,' he murmured, then laughed softly, deep inside his throat, as if fully aware that the kisses he was feathering against the silken, exposed curve of her shoulder were jabbing delicious thrills of terror along every nerve. 'Do you regret the absence of male hunger, *carita de angel*?' he chided thickly. 'Very well, as you appear to cherish a yearning to be wooed, then by all means let us have a clause to that effect written into our contract!'

CHAPTER EIGHT

WEARING the simple white dress Dr Ribero had brought with him from the Reserve, and with it the necklace of brilliant blue beads that Sabelita had insisted must be kept about her person as protection against the 'evil eye', Frances exchanged marriage vows with the Conde in low, faltering responses that drifted like a sigh into the silent interior of a private chapel inside which sad-eyed plaster Madonnas and saints with painted expressions of extreme melancholy had looked down upon generations of family baptisms.

On Dr Ribero's supportive arm she had walked up to the altar rails where the Conde had stood waiting, and amid an atmosphere redolent with the perfume of massed *albahaca* blossoms had promised like a spirit bewitched to love, honour and obey the man who needed a wife to bear him a child, one who could be paraded like the trophies his Moorish ancestor had paraded in order to communicate contempt of neighbouring Spaniards who had dared to oppose his will.

'May I say, Condesa, how very proud I am to have been asked to act as a stand-in for my friend, your late father?' Bernardo Ribero beamed at the bride, looking as bemused as a child caught up in some grown-ups' procession. 'At the risk of being thought presumptuous, I must state—as I am certain he would if he were present—that no father

could hope to place his daughter into better,
kinder or more thoughtful hands than those of El
Conde! May *el Buen Dios* bless you both,' he
concluded simply, 'and also the marriage that I
have been privileged to witness this day.'

Frances smiled her thanks, unwilling to speak in
case words should break the trance-like state of
bewitchment in which she had existed ever since
the moment the Conde had forced from her
crushed, passion-inflamed lips the confession that
she loved him, adored him, that her rapturously
awakened body had been seduced by an insane
longing to belong to him.

'Thank you, Bernardo, for your support and for
your good wishes. Knowing the little amount of
time you can afford to spare at this season of the
year, I have instructed the pilot to have the
helicopter ready for an immediate return flight to
the Reserve. So sorry you cannot join us for a
celebration lunch,' he concluded with what
sounded to Frances like an abrupt dismissal,
'however, I'm certain my wife will second my
invitation to pay us a visit at some early date.'

Unaware of tension that was causing her fingers
to contract around the stems of *albahaca* flowers
threaded through her bouquet, Frances waited
with the Conde outside the chapel until Dr
Ribero's departing figure had faded to a speck in
the distance. Then, her senses reeling from the
effect of potent perfume rising in a cloud from
flowers employed by gypsies to ease the pain of
unrequited love, she raised reproachful eyes towards her unsmiling, totally unrepentant husband.

'Sometimes, Rom,' his name seemed to stick for

an anguished second in her throat, 'I wonder if you realise how aggressive you can appear to those who offer you love or friendship?'

'I learnt the habit from nature, *cara,*' he returned, making no pretence of misunderstanding. 'Big birds eat little birds, little birds eat insects, insects eat grubs. I never seek affection,' he shrugged, 'therefore I see no reason why I should feel guilty about those who offer it too readily.'

'You dismiss friendship and affection because you are not prepared to give anything in return,' Frances murmured sadly, pained by this brief insight into the heart and mind of the husband she had resigned herself to loving even though she knew he had no love to give her in return.

As if sensing a little of the dejection being felt by his new bride, he gently tilted her chin with a forefinger and gazed deeply into eyes reflecting the moist blue loveliness of violets.

'I wear no mask for you, Frances,' he grated. 'But because I lost my heart once and swore never to do so again, it does not follow that I am incapable of emotion—only that I refuse to become passion's slave. The truest comparison I can make is that of a man who, having recovered from a bout of fever, is still prone to regular attacks, yet has been rendered immune to dangerous complications.'

She blushed wildly, feeling cheapened by the memory of how his experienced touch had plucked from her previously untouched emotions sweet, hesitant notes, swift trills, and rippling trebles that had scaled higher and higher towards the top octave, yet stopped just short of an ultimate, earth-shattering crescendo. When the music had died to a whisper she had felt shocked, startled, and bewildered by her reactions, but the Conde had left her in no doubt of his delight in the discovery of a virgin who had turned wanton at his touch, of an abstemious Eve who had sipped the wine of love and found its potency addictive.

His kisses had awakened her to love, a love that was unafraid, imposing no conditions. In spite of warnings from her father who, in the past, had become concerned about her tendency to return in abundance every overture of friendship even from those whose motives he had often declared suspect, she had offered unreservedly every ounce of emotion that was inside of her to give—like an overlooked flower full of stored-up sweetness she had opened petals of innocence to a foraging bee and had been drained dry. Many times since she had sought to justify her reckless, completely uncharacteristic surrender to passion, but had finally been forced to grab at the straw of an excuse contained in the Conde's statement, *'Some say that to live here in Andalusia is to be slowly born again—sometimes as a stranger totally unknown, completely different from one's normal self!'*

As if moved to pity by the dazed-eyed girl who had been transformed from a bride into a wife by a brief, hasty ceremony that might truthfully have been classed as furtive, the Conde took hold of her hand, raised it to his lips, then slowly and carefully kissed each frozen fingertip.

'I'm sorry you have been denied all the pomp and

ceremony every bride is entitled to expect on her wedding day, *cara*.'

'It doesn't matter,' she swallowed painfully, braving his look with eyes saddened by the lie.

'But it does,' he contradicted gravely. 'The two best days of a woman's life should be the day that she marries and the day that she gives birth to her first child. Fortunately, there is a second ceremony that must be performed before we can be considered married in the eyes of my gypsy family. You may find their customs strange, but I can promise that there will be no shortage of happiness and good wishes, for they have taken you to their hearts with an enthusiasm I would not have believed possible.'

'I have gained great satisfaction from my involvement with my appealing, responsive, intelligent pupils, and had even begun to imagine that a bond of friendship had been forged between myself and their parents,' she reproached, her dignity offended by his incredulity.

'Your reasoning was well founded,' he answered gravely. 'However, gypsies—even more so than their Spanish bull-rearing neighbours—are fanatically insistent upon keeping their blood strain pure. In spite of my family's mingling of Moorish, Spanish and Romany blood, for generations past each firstborn son has been hailed by the gypsies as one of their own, basing their claim upon an inherited physical characteristic shared right up until the present day by descendants of young Isabella, the first Romany Condesa.' Absently, he brushed a hand across a temple where a sable wing of hair glistened with the silver-bright markings of the imperial eagle. 'Because of the very special relationship that has existed between my family and their tribe, the gypsies have tolerated, albeit resentfully, a succession of Condesas whose Spanish blood has offended against the strict gypsy law that requires a union between a gypsy and non-gypsy to be punished by automatic exclusion from the tribe. But in your case, my *giganilla*, they are prepared to break with customs relating to marriage that are as old as time by offering to perform the rites of a Romany marriage for the benefit of one who is not of their race.'

Her heart seemed to flutter in her throat as she sought for words to express the feeling of warmth and comfort she had gained from the knowledge that, at a time when she was feeling deprived of the support of family and friends, she was about to be adopted by the friendly, welcoming tribe.

Apparently finding the expressions chasing across her pale face as easy to read as an open book, he tipped a finger under her chin and looked deeply into her eyes still dazed with the solemnity of the recent ceremony, before offering guidance to his confused child-bride.

'I must warn you, Frances,' he frowned, 'that once you are adopted by the gypsies you will be obliged to follow their traditions, to submit to laws that demand prompt obedience. For instance, every Romany wife is expected to show absolute submission to her husband. Might such a law make me appear more of a warder in your eyes? Even cause you eventually to look upon your home as a prison?'

Bravely, she countered his attack of probing

with a look of honesty that might have drawn a
twinge of compassion from a heart of stone.

'Prison is a place where happiness cannot thrive;
a place of rogues, and most of all, a place where
one is kept against one's will. My dearest wish was
granted,' she admitted simply, 'when you asked me
to remain here with you.'

When he bent his head to place a grateful kiss
upon her downcast mouth the world suddenly
dissolved into a warm, golden orb sparkling with
brilliant sunshine.

'Let us go, Condesa,' he mocked her swift rise of
colour. 'As if the acquisition of one title were not
sufficient, you will soon be dubbed my *Bori Rani*!'

During the breathtaking ride in an open-topped
car towards the ravine where the gypsies' caves
were situated, Frances' spirits rose high as her
wind-swept hair glowed sparkling as the glances
cast in her direction by dark eyes lit by a glint of
appreciation that seemed to indicate that he found
her happiness infectious. As the car breasted a rise,
then dipped to begin racing along the floor of the
ravine, the sound of music rose in the air to greet
them, a wildly welcoming salutation of strumming
guitars, frenzied fiddles and clicking castanets.

The moment the car braked to a standstill on
the edge of a clearing massed with flowers of every
available colour, entwined around the branches of
trees, crammed into large earthenware pitchers, set
in vases ranged down the centre of trestle tables,
even strewn upon the ground to form a fragrant
carpet beneath the feet of the bride and
bridegroom, the entire gypsy tribe rushed to greet
them.

A roar of appreciation ripped from their throats when the man they regarded as their chief lifted his bride from her seat and then swung her aloft to display her blushing confusion to the tribe before setting her lightly upon her feet.

'Droboy tum Romale!' The greeting was shouted by a crowd of gypsies massed colourful as exotic butterflies, women and children wearing dresses of flaming pinks, vivid orange, yellow and innumerable shades of red, sleek-fitting and flounced below the knee, dotted and striped, flowered and sequined, with low-cut, off-the-shoulder necklines filled in with golden chains to match dangling earrings, bracelets, and rings crammed one on each finger and, in the case of those who were barefoot, even on some toes. And men looking no less festive in colourful, wide-sleeved shirts worn beneath velvet waistcoats trimmed around the edges with gold coins; satin cummerbunds, and bright neckerchiefs knotted inside the collars of shirts slashed open to the waist.

'Nais tuke!' Frances' heart turned a somersault at the surprising discovery that the Conde was capable of displaying a wide, engaging grin, then soared almost out of orbit when, with her hand in his, he raised their arms together in a gesture of mutual commitment before proffering simply,

'I come to present my *gitanilla*, my little gypsy girl, and your future Bori Rani!'

In spite of her endeavour to retain a tight clasp upon his hand, she felt herself being swept away when the crowd of gypsies descended and then divided into two separate male and female factions. As she was urged in the direction of a tent that had been erected in total seclusion on the far edge of the clearing she sped a look of puzzlement across the bobbing sea of heads and was rewarded with a wave of encouragement from her husband, who seemed to have become involved in some sort of mild-tempered argument with his voluble gypsy brothers.

'Step in here, Bori Rani, if you please.' Sabelita was holding the flap door of the tent open wide.

Giving in to the urgings of the widely smiling, elbow-nudging women, she responded to Sabelita's request, then gasped for breath when immediately she entered the tent she was assailed by a warm, heavy wave of perfume wafting from *albahaca* blossoms lining every inch of the tent from floor to ceiling.

'Heavens!' she gasped, overwhelmed by their beauty but almost overcome by the strongly narcotic effect of their perfume. 'If I'm to be forced to stay inside this tent for any length of time I must have more air,' she insisted, hastening to open the closed flapdoor. 'Why have I been brought here, Sabelita?' she puzzled, 'And why does everyone keep addressing me as *Bori Rani*?'

'Because you are a great lady, wife of our gypsy gentleman, Romany Rye,' Sabelita explained patiently.

'I a great lady? I don't think so,' Frances laughed aloud, feeling unnerved yet flattered.

'A gypsy is guided only by his own instincts. No one, not even Romany Rye, could order the members of my tribe to scour the woods for the rare, secreted flower of matrimonial bliss if they had not thought you deserving. We need no gift of second sight to recognise the love you feel in your heart for our children as well as for our chief. Our tribe is poor, but we wished to show our gratitude and did so with the only power in our means, a power gained through knowledge of plants and their uses that has been gathered from the four corners of the earth and passed down through untold generations. This is our wedding gift to you, Bori Rani,' her wave encompassed the curtain of white, star-shaped flowers lining the walls of the tent, 'the herb with magical properties that will transport you this night to paradise where you will conceive a fine, healthy son!'

Aware from past experience how little there was to be gained from arguing a point with Sabelita, Frances bowed to the inevitable, even to the point of donning the dress made by the women of the tribe especially for her gypsy wedding. Whether guided by luck or by a flair for matching colour to character, the soft blue material they had chosen cast deep violet shadows over her grey eyes so that they looked mysterious and infinitely appealing. The design of the dress followed their favourite theme of tight-fitting bodice dipping low to meet a ruffled ankle-length skirt that had a slit up the middle to allow a glimpse of rounded knees and to provide a tempting display of shapely calves, and slender, finely boned ankles.

The one thing that Frances found troubling was a neckline cut low enough to make her feel brazen whenever she glanced down upon milk-white curves that seemed in danger of overflowing a band of blue velvet so tightly constricting it had the effect of making her breasts swell, curve, then plunge downward to form a deep, mysterious, glance-enticing valley. After futile seconds spent trying to tug the bodice upwards, she frowned and gnawed her bottom lip.

'Sabelita, I can't possibly wear this dress, it makes me feel too ... too ...'

'Seductive?' Sabelita suggested slyly, casting a look of approval over curves bulging over the top of her dress like milk-white pomegranates. 'To please a woman in the first place, a man must undress her,' she chuckled, 'therefore it does not make sense for a bride to make the task more difficult for her bridegroom on their wedding night!'

Frances swung round, her cheeks made fiery by the earthy remark, intending to insist upon being provided with a shawl, but was just in time to see Sabelita hurrying out of the tent to make way for a strange gypsy male.

'Would you kindly not walk into my tent unannounced,' she began sharply, then took a quick step backwards when she realised that the flashing-eyed, sable-haired man wearing tight breeches tucked into the tops of knee-length leather boots, and a silken shirt with wide sleeves gathered tightly at the wrists, was the aloof, rarely-smiling Conde.

But whereas she was startled, he appeared stunned as silently he eyed her appearance, his gaze travelling slowly from the crown of her silvery blonde head down to the toes of buckled blue slippers, then swiftly and inevitably upwards, to linger with an intentness that caused her body to feel suffused by a hot embarrassed scorch.

'*Madre de Dios!*' he murmured with an audacity that was pure Romany. 'Have I the courage to flaunt such temptation before a tribe of macho gypsy males? You look so delectable, *mi gitanilla*, I feel it would be unfair of me to tantalise men accustomed to a diet of boiled turnip with the sight of a tender young fowl dressed and prepared for my own private relishment.'

A tender-skinned chicken could not have reacted more sensitively to the fiery blast of embarrassment that sent heat racing through Frances' veins as she was made to feel plucked, trussed and dressed in a manner designed to add savour and piquancy to his jaded appetite.

'I'll save you the trouble of having to make a decision,' she lashed out in temper. 'I will not be paraded in front of your gypsy friends wearing a dress that's positively indecent!'

'Bared breasts appear beautiful to honest gypsy eyes,' he rebuked coolly, increasing her aggravation by training his glance upon breasts supplying pounding proof of outraged modesty. 'They scorn man's invented indecencies and accept as one of the bounties of Nature the unselfconscious beauty of girls washing their naked bodies at the riverside. As a matter of fact,' he glinted wickedly, 'I am the only person whose behaviour is likely to cause adverse comment. According to custom, I ought to be using this interlude to round off my education by seeking the counsel of older and wiser members of the tribe who are accustomed to being approached by novice bridegrooms in search of practical explanations designed to help them achieve a state of conjugal bliss.'

'But you have no need, of course!' Frances tilted recklessly. 'No doubt you feel you've gained ample knowledge of an experience enjoyed until its pleasures have become exhausted!'

When he strode towards her the blossom-scented air became agitated, encompassing them both in a cloud of heady sensuous perfume.

'You have so much to give, child heart,' he murmured, scanning her naked shoulders with a look akin to that of a starving man who has been invited to a banquet. 'Your cup of innocence is full, mine has been drained, and when a man is thirsty enough, *cara*, he will accept any drink, however innocuous the brew!'

Frances shuddered with sudden exquisite pleasure when he pulled her into his arms and began stroking a caressing hand along the length of her spine, then felt aching need building up inside her as he began plucking upon her nerves like the strings of a harp, tracing every curve and swell of her body before stamping a fiery, branding kiss upon the cool tender curve of her shoulder. She sighed immediate surrender, arching closer to slide trembling hands inside a shirt falling open across a broad chest with muscles knotting beneath skin rippling smooth as polished mahogany beneath her stroking fingers.

'Señor Conde! Señora Condesa!'

Sabelita's voice acted like a douche of cold water upon Frances' fevered emotions, wrenching her out of the arms of the man who had chosen her not as a man chooses a wife, but as a lonely eagle might pounce upon any available mate.

Unaware that she was intruding, Sabelita

bustled inside the tent like an over-anxious duenna, then halted suddenly, obviously conscious of the Conde's resentment and the powerful sense of *comova*, a term gypsies used to express intense physical desire.

When the Conde swung on his heel to condemn her appearance with a glint of icy displeasure she backed away, but then, as if stiffening her resolve to ensure that conventions were observed, she drew herself erect and reprimanded with the asperity of a duenna conscious of her responsibilities towards a lady of high rank,

'Everything is ready. The tribe waits impatiently for the ceremony to begin!'

Grateful for her reprieve, Frances made a rush towards the door of the tent, but was pulled up short by a whiplash grip upon her wrist.

'Sabelita may have taken upon herself the duties of a eunuch in a harem,' he derided coldly, 'nevertheless, I refuse to allow you to run like an outraged virgin from my presence.'

Withering Sabelita with a look, he commanded with the arrogance of a gypsy chief who used a triple-thonged whip as his badge of office. 'Go! The wedding ceremony will begin when *I* decide.'

But as swiftly as Sabelita shot outside the tent, he regained control of his temper, the Romany rake usurped by a familiarly aloof grandee with a proud manner, expressionless features, and eyes dark and fathomless as night—with only an occasional spitting spark to remind her that the fire she had so foolishly helped to kindle had not been extinguished, merely dampened and left dangerously smouldering.

CHAPTER NINE

WHEN Rom stepped outside the tent dressed as his tribe had longed to see him in the traditional garb of a Romany chief with a heavy golden ring of rank prominently displayed upon the hand gripping a triple-thonged whip of authority, a great cheer of approval rose to greet him, and the girl whose shy, gentle eyes were incapable of concealing the love she felt for the man holding her close as a shadow to his side.

Two youths strolled forward to meet them, strumming a sweet serenade upon gypsy violins as they sang praises of the bride's charm and beauty and of her lover's devotion.

Nervously, she quivered when the swaying, smiling crowd parted to admit Floure's youngest daughter bearing a coronet of flowers upon a velvet cushion, but managed to stoop gracefully when the child disposed of the cushion and lifted the beribboned garland high, indicating that she wished to place it like a crown upon the bride's head.

'Take the red cord, also,' Rom instructed when Frances hesitated, uncertain whether or not to accept the child's second offering of a skein of red string, 'then hand it to me, thereby signifying your consent to our marriage.'

Immediately Rom accepted the gift from his blushing bride a murmur of approval rippled through their audience, which then began reassembling to form a guard of honour that wended out of sight towards the perimeter of the clearing. At the sound of a rapid, throbbing drumroll, Frances felt a shiver of trepidation chasing up her spine, but as if her sense of panic had been communicated to him, Rom gave her hand a squeeze and tucked it into the crook of his elbow before guiding her forward to begin a long, slow procession between the ranks of eager, expectant-looking gypsies.

'What's about to happen?' she whispered urgently as they came within sight of a carpeted dais strewn with flower petals that had one large wooden chair set like a throne in its centre.

'Even Gentiles must be aware of the legendary gypsy blood marriage, during which ritual incisions are made in each wrist so that the blood of both parties can mingle? Don't look so shocked,' he laughed beneath his breath, throwing an arm around her shoulders so that her look of startled incredulity was hidden from sight. 'I promise that you will feel no pain, Culvato's dagger is too sharp, his regard for you too high, to permit him to inflict anything more than a slight discomfort.'

Beginning to wonder if she was the victim of some weird, hallucinatory dream, Frances concentrated her mind upon urging her reluctant feet to tread the petal-strewn path leading up to the dais that had taken on the appearance of a sacrificial altar where the swarthy-skinned Culvato, his beard neatly trimmed and pointed, was standing, dagger poised, waiting like Diabolus to admit her damned spirit into his demoniac possession.

Without the protective shield of Rom's arm

around her shoulders, without his powerfully
reassuring presence and murmured words of
encouragement, she could not have endured the
rituals performed during the very old marriage
ceremony that the Romanies held sacred.

Though no more than a large wooden chair, the
'throne' upon which she was kept symbolically
isolated by a loosely-hung chain draped across her
lap lost none of its regality as she sat trembling
upon its rush-woven seat, her wide, apprehensive
eyes trained upon Culvato's silver-bladed dagger
glinting wickedly as razor-sharp edges were
whetted by glancing sunrays.

Rom was standing behind her chair with a
consoling hand resting lightly upon her shoulder
when the drumroll died to a faint background
rumbling and the tribe fell silent, crowding around
the dais with a sudden air of solemnity that she
found unnerving.

Savage-looking, stiff-haired dogs that prowled
continuously around the cave houses ceased
howling and barking, rollicking children were
rebuked into silence, tethered horses stopped
snorting and neighing, and the pungent smell of
burning wood drifted over the clearing from thin
corkscrews of blue smoke rising from campfires,
when Rom's loud, clear voice resounded with a
formality that warned Frances that the mysterious
rites were about to begin.

'By your leave, gypsy men and youths, this is
Romanes calling upon you to witness his marriage
to Frances!'

Coins, bracelets and earrings jangled, voluminous skirts rustled as the gypsy audience pressed

forward, nodding permission to Culvato to respond in their name.

'By your leave, Romanes, this is Culvato agreeing on behalf of his tribe to perform the necessary rites, and also to act as witness to your marriage to Frances!' Solemnly, he broke a piece of bread into two pieces, sprinkled salt on each of the fragments, then handed one each to the bride and bridegroom, miming instructions to Frances to exchange her portion with Rom before eating. Then as she chewed for a second before forcing the bread down her constricted throat, he intoned sternly,

'When you are tired of this bread and this salt, you will be tired of one another!'

During the shower of rice grains that followed the symbolic bestowal of wealth and prosperity, Frances felt the hand of some unseen person closing around her left wrist, levering it upwards until it was level with the left wrist of Rom. She did not resist, but kept her wide eyes, riveted upon the point of the silver dagger Culvato began lowering towards a pale blue vein outstanding on her wrist, pulsating in time with her rapidly pounding heartbeats.

The incision, when it came, felt like the merest pinprick, yet her blood spurted as if leaping with joy towards the dark red stream gushing from Rom's lacerated wrist. A split second later their wrists were clamped and bound tightly together with strips of cloth so that their life-blood could mingle, turning two separate entities into one.

Shaken to the core by a physical communion so intimate she felt possessed, her virgin body invaded by the blood of the rapacious Moor who had used a young slave girl to slake his loneliness and to share his bondage of self-imposed isolation, she stared into the darkly brooding eyes of her Romany husband, wondering whether, even as they remained bound, giving and accepting the blood of each other, his thoughts were dwelling upon Maria, the girl he had loved passionately enough to ask her to become his wife, the one whose rejection had turned an adoring youth into a cold, embittered man.

'May your clothes rip and wear out, but may you live in good health and in happy fulfilment!'

Culvato's final blessing coincided with the removal of the cloth binding their wrists. Reluctantly, Frances withdrew her arm to enable Floure to wipe her wrist clean, then stared with disbelief at skin that was unblemished except for a faint red scar.

'We use a lotion distilled from herbs to stop the bleeding instantly,' Floure responded to her look of puzzlement. 'Tomorrow you will need to search for evidence of the incision.'

Floure's retreat from the dais with her bottle of herbal magic seemed to signify the conclusion of the ceremony and the commencement of high-spirited revelry that began with a congratulatory roar, a surge of hand-shaking, back-slapping good wishes, then progressed into a skirt-swirling, hip-jerking, foot-tapping furore of dancing as exhilarated gypsies endeavoured to keep pace with the lively tempo of gypsy music.

'Prepare yourself for an exhausting day,' Rom warned, pulling Frances behind the trunk of a tree that had a canopy of low-slung branches offering a promise of comparative seclusion. 'The ceremonial celebrations to honour special guests, known to the gypsies as *"Pashiv"*, has been known to last for two or three days!'

Perhaps the Cante Hondo was too loud, yet Frances could not help but suspect that he had seized upon the loudness of Spanish gypsy music as an excuse to pull her into his arms and to feather his lips across a burning ear-lobe.

'You looked so scared at the sight of the plunging silver dagger,' he mused with the benevolence of a man in complete charge of his emotions. 'I'm sorry you found the ceremony such an ordeal. Romanies excel at wringing the last drop of drama out of their rituals, they scorn subtlety—not for them the wisdom of serpents and the gentleness of doves, every story they tell has to be told in full, with every detail outlined until the mind is peaceful and the imagination satisfied. They make love as if making war,' his lips swept a trail of fire across her cheek, then hovered to breathe against her startled mouth, 'but we shall manage without the weapons of war, my *gitanilla*, provided we can provide plenty of fuel, for without wood the fire will die!'

With a heart as heavy as stone she endured his deeply probing kiss, wondering why fate could not have been kind enough to decree that she should marry a man who loved her, instead of merely mating her with the man she loved.

Instinct warned her to tread warily, to show gratitude for any morsel of affection he might choose to toss her way, but with his blood running wild in her veins, with the taste of bread upon her tongue and the sting of salt upon her lips, she felt an urgent craving for more.

When she pulled out of his arms Rom showed surprise at the first sign of resistance she had ever demonstrated.

'Are you still so much in love with Maria that all you can offer me is the sort of relationship that once existed between tyrant and slave?' she charged shakily, not caring if he should lie, so long as she could redeem a little of her self-respect.

Immediately his expression froze into a mask of hauteur she knew that she had spoken unwisely.

'I offered you a bargain,' he reminded her coldly. 'A deal in which love had no part to play. And as for Maria,' his voice suddenly grated, 'my feelings for her are irrelevant, buried in the past.'

'A past that refuses to go away,' she continued recklessly, knowing herself foolish for loving him so. 'Maria is a ghost in your life that nobody talks about and few ever see, yet her spirit still lives inside the broken-down shrine you call a heart!'

'*Dios!*' he spat, looking angry enough to break his whip of authority across her stiffly-held spine. 'I offered you wealth and comfort in exchange for a son, no more and no less! Remember *always*,' he stressed with a look so contemptuous she wanted to curl up and die, 'that part of the duty of a wife is to assuage her husband's hunger, but though duty may force me to eat at your table, I shall decide for myself where I shall dine!'

Wild berries, mushrooms, nettles and herbs were simmering with the juices of games and fowl in huge iron cauldrons positioned above campfires ringing the clearing. Hedgehogs encased in clay were roasting slowly on flat, white-hot stones sunk into the ground to form primitive ovens, and as it was the beginning of a *Patshiva*, a great ceremonial occasion, beer and wine had replaced the gypsies' favourite drink of sparkling water and tea that they managed to drink boiling hot by pouring it, a little at a time, into a saucer and then drinking it with a noisy lack of fastidiousness.

Nervously twisting through her fingers the strand of blue beads Sabelita had promised would bestow 'a thousand blessings', Frances allowed Rom to lead her towards a seat provided by the tribe for the bridal pair, a high-backed, wooden love-seat providing just sufficient room for two to sit in close proximity. When Rom indicated that he wished her to sit down she breathed in deeply, foolishly attempting to shrink her slender frame into the far corner of the seat in case he should notice her weak trembling. But immediately he joined her, she felt engulfed, vitally aware of the ripple of muscles where their thighs touched, of rock-hard biceps brushing against her cheek, of sensual heat emanating in waves from the virile, power-packed body of the husband who expected no more of a wife than that she should provide him with sons.

Shivering, uncontrollable as ague, erupted through her tense body when she realised with a sudden sense of shock how quickly Sabelita's unlikely prophecy had come to pass.

'It is written in the stars, in the sand, and in the movements of the planets,' she had declared, *'that you and Romany Rye will take bread and salt!'*

Did Romanies possess some magical power that enabled them to manipulate the future? Or was society right to condemn them as smooth-tongued tricksters who bewitched money from the pockets of the gullible by filling their ears with promises of luck and the state of Utopian happiness yearned for by every mortal?

'Why are you shivering? Surely you are not cold?'

Frances cringed from the arm Rom slid around her shoulders, convinced that he was not acting out of concern for herself but demonstrating affection merely for the benefit of their audience. 'Would you like me to fetch a shawl to put around your shoulders?' He frowned, kindling a spark amongst her charred emotions by stroking an exploratory palm across her naked shoulders.

'I suppose, as I am now a chattel, I must do whatever my master commands,' she responded coldly, deciding that she might as well be hanged for a sheep as for a lamb. 'As you have already stated a liking for nudity, I'm surprised by your willingness to allow a veil to be drawn across the spectacle of a slave dressed to please her owner.'

She knew by the flicker in his dark eyes that he was angry, yet onlookers who noticed her wild rush of colour could have been forgiven for assuming that Rom was paying flattering attention to his bride when he bent his head low to murmur,

'I am fond of women, I like their company, I adore seeing their femininity emphasised by voluptuous clothes designed, as a trap is designed, to display just a sufficient amount of bait to attract and to ensnare the unwary. I enjoy being just a

little in love with, and spoiling, women who excite
my interest. But I have never expected nor
demanded servitude in exchange. In fact, Frances,'
a muscle jerked in his suddenly tightened jaw, 'up
until recently I had never been made to feel a
tyrant, nor have I ever before had to curb an
impulse to inflict a salutary beating. I suspect that
taking you for a wife might be similar to making a
pet of a tiger cub—one can never be certain if one
is master!'

At that precise moment, as their eyes were
locked in combat, a male elder of the tribe was
escorted into the clearing and left standing alone,
waiting with his head thrown back until the entire
tribe had lapsed into silence. When he began
singing, unaccompanied, his quavering but still
powerful voice sounded to Frances like the prayer
chants of Islam, a flamenco, very Arabic in
flavour, which she gathered from Rom's whispered
translation told the ancient story of how gypsies
had migrated into Spain from India, their original
homeland, the birthplace of a culture Romanies
had preserved in secret during their centuries of
nomadic wandering.

The old man sobbed his grief for a race branded
as outsiders, wailed and wrung his hands as he
mourned the ignorance shown by people who
levelled hatred and envy upon gypsies who insisted
upon remaining separate, different, and refused to
conform to the values of others. Many pious
references were made to the goddess Kali, the
Hindu goddess who had travelled with them
through time and remained alive in their myths
and legends. Then as the ancient ballad drew to a

close, the old man's voice grew deep with emotion
as he lifted his hands towards heaven, pleading for
justice to be shown to nomads cast out of lands
because of an undeserved reputation for stealing,
plundering and trickery, whose daughters had to
dance, whose sons had to become musicians before
they could become integrated, accepted by Gentiles
whose hearts and minds could only be invaded by
unique, artistic talent.

'Not all flamenco songs are devoted to history
and politics,' Rom assured Frances under cover of
tumultuous applause. 'Just like their life, gypsy
music is full of contradictions. Melancholy must
be purged before gaiety can emerge—a very special
quality of gaiety, vibrant as an electric shock, that
is communicated to all hearts by their passion for
dancing. Never was a gypsy born that was not
born to dance,' he mused, 'and especially a
Spanish gypsy,' he told her in a tone so low and
lacking in bite it caused her heart to flip right over.
'Later, *querida*, after the feasting is finished and
night has fallen, you will be called upon to display
your talents, to prove that even a cool, poised
English girl can dance as if she had a little Spanish
honey in her hips.'

'But I can't dance,' she protested, 'I've never
had any opportunity to try!'

'There's nothing to it,' he insisted with a glint of
Moorish wickedness. 'Gypsy children are taught a
few basic rules, then the rest is left to natural
ability.

*Do not look at your feet to see if you are doing
the steps properly but keep your head up and look
about you confidently. Make sure that you have a*

clean handkerchief, but do not use it more than is absolutely necessary. If stockings and shoes are being worn, see that the first do not slip down and that the second are well polished and never allowed to become soiled.'

Rom's aggravation seemed to wane as gradually as the sinking sun, so that by the time it had dipped below the horizon his mood was as mellow as darkness flung like a cloak over the clearing scented with the heady perfume of crushed flower petals, glowing with the warmth of flaring campfires, vital and exciting as the music of guitars and gypsy violins that played havoc with the senses, setting feet tapping, bodies swaying, hearts racing to keep up with its wild, exhilarating beat.

The gypsies had eaten their fill of thick game stew and hedgehog cooked to a turn so that when the clay was removed the prickles remained embedded in the crust and the meat was ready to be served upon plate-sized leaves.

Rom had noticed Frances' start of revulsion at the sight of hedgehog bellies being split open and the entrails disposed of at the very last moment before portions were distributed. But although he had jeered at her squeamish inability to taste even a morsel of the large helping she had been served, he had surreptitiously scooped her portion on to his plate so that their hosts would not be offended by her rejection of a dish they had proudly assured here was 'good enough for a queen to eat without salt'.

They were watching a nuptial dance, a performance enacted by six betrothed couples that had begun by portraying the shy, tentative approach at a girl and boy's first meeting, had advanced slowly towards the quick tempo of mutual attraction, then escalated suddenly into a burst of eye-flashing, posturing, passionate flirtation, every gesture and movement sending out signals of desire, of sexual arousal that could be assuaged only by the magical intimacy of marriage.

Frances watched breathlessly, gripped by the savage beauty of the performance, unaware that the ritual dance of seduction had any bearing upon her own coldblooded marriage of convenience until, when excitement was at its peak, the music ceased as suddenly as the dancers' tempestuously tapping feet and a whole audience of dark, expectant eyes swivelled towards herself and Rom.

'It is up to us, as newlyweds, to supply a fitting climax,' Rom explained, pulling her to her feet. 'Just relax, *querida*, and try to look as happy as a bride should look when she knows the pinnacle of happiness is almost within reach.'

His words made no sense to her panic-ridden mind, nor did it seem reasonable of him to expect—having already been told that she could not dance—that she would accompany him willingly on to a stage where they would be expected to conclude the ritual dance with some sort of dramatic finale.

Cringing with shyness, she was forced to accompany Rom into the centre of the clearing where she stood on leaden feet, directing an imploring plea to be rescued from the nightmare situation. But, looking completely impenitent, Rom refused to be moved, even demonstrated his

eagerness to act out the role of enamoured
bridegroom by gripping a waist that fitted as
neatly into his palm as the handle of a whip and
pulling her close enough to feel the kick of his
heartbeats, the animal sensuality of muscles
rippling beneath the shirt clinging close to his
frame as a silken pelt.

The magic of his touch drew from her lips a sigh
of surrender, dispersed from her mind all
consciousness of others, so that as she trembled
within the circle of his arms, feeling the glow of
campfires licking heat across the pale, exposed
skin of her shoulders, seeing the reflection of
flames flickering in the depths of eyes black as sin,
she felt ringed by fire, held fast in the arms of a
Romany devil hellbent upon introducing yet
another slave into his Satanic harem.

When his grip increased in urgency she tried to
draw away, but then, as if demons of sorcery had
been summoned to his aid, violins began playing a
sweet, pagan, insidious psalm of temptation.
Instinctively, intent as a priestess moving through
some holy ritual, she responded to his guidance,
swaying when he swayed, matching each of his
steps with an inherent grace of movement that
made her appear ethereal, a sweetly serious cherub
drifting languorously, gliding, swirling, ebbing and
flowing within a pale blue cloud of enchantment.

Perhaps it was the magical influence of
midnight, or the brilliance of stars reflected in her
entranced eyes that was responsible for Rom's
rasped-in breath, his sudden jerk to a standstill.

'When you decide to give you always give
generously, my *gitanilla*,' he admitted roughly.

'With you there are no half measures either of passion or patience. It must have been someone with a nature as sweet as your own that inspired the gypsy belief: *"Don del tut o nai shai dela tut wi o vast"*—he who willingly gives you one finger will also give you the whole hand!'

With a suddenness that barely left her time to emerge from her euphoric daze or, more mercifully, for her mind to dwell for more than a split second upon the significance of the actions of every member of the tribe rushing to range themselves into a route leading directly up to the entrance of the flower-lined bridal tent, Rom swept her off her feet and began carrying her in triumph along the path of destiny, being assailed on all sides by enthusiastic yells of encouragement and earthy predictions of nuptial bliss from gypsies who saw beauty in nubile nudity and considered the act of making love as natural and as necessary to life as breathing . . .

When he laid her down upon a pile of silk-covered cushions stuffed with dried, scented herbs gathered from wild woodland dells and lush, green meadows, Frances' pale, stricken face immediately assumed the vivid pink blush of a shy, startled flamingo. Ranged around the walls of the tent were piles of wedding presents—woven baskets, hand-thrown pottery, lace-trimmed pillowcases, frilled petticoats and a layette, complete with waterproof sheet, spread out in front of a crib holding a plaster figure of the Holy Child with the crown of blossoms she had discarded earlier in the day clutched between plump, dimpled fingers.

'How beautiful you look, *camomescra*, with

your eyes reflecting the misty blue colour of
rosemary in full bloom,' Rom husked, haughty
hidalgo completely routed by the passionate,
romantic Romany.

Forgetting her vortex of shame, her resolve to
hold fast to a few tattered remnants of self-respect,
Frances offered her lips to be crushed, as
sweetness had been crushed from *albahaca* petals
so that the bridal tent could be flooded with the
heady incense said to have been favoured by
Aphrodite, goddess of sensual love . . .

CHAPTER TEN

Cautiously, Frances wriggled her toes in an attempt to relieve cramped leg muscles, at the same time being careful to keep her binoculars trained upon the nest she had discovered after days spent monitoring the to-ing and fro-ing of a pair of Spanish imperial eagles.

The first sighting had been made by one of the estate workers who had then reported to Rom the approximate location of the nest. He, in turn, had arranged for a hide to be erected in the woods, close enough to allow her to study the eagles' habits yet far enough away from the nesting birds to remain undisturbed.

As they were moving towards a season during which a profusion of *ferias* were due to be held, a time of round-the-clock festival fever marked by daily bullfights, cattle fairs, dancing, singing in the streets and fairground razzmatazz, the gypsy dancers and singers were to be much in demand in nearby towns and villages, therefore schooling had been temporarily curtailed—which was why, for the past fortnight, while the children were on holiday, Frances had been able to return each day to keep vigil at the nest site, to watch the birds moving through the ritual of courtship and the early stages of egg laying.

She stiffened when above the sounds of chirping

birds and the rustling of small, unseen animals in
the dry undergrowth, she imagined she detected
the sound of a car being driven along the road
skirting the edge of the wood. She glanced at her
watch, knowing that it was too early for the arrival
of the estate worker who dropped her off each
morning with her binoculars, thermos flask full of
coffee, and a sufficient number of sandwiches to
keep hunger at bay until she was transported back
to the Palacio in time for the evening meal.

Once, Rom had promised—rather idly, she had
thought—to share her vigil for a day. But during
the two weeks that had elapsed he had not
bothered to put in an appearance.

In spite of the warm humidity inside the hide
she shivered and turned aside to grope for her
pack of sandwiches, hoping to assuage hunger
gnawing deep inside her, even though she was
perfectly well aware that the pangs knotting her
stomach until she felt faint, that caused her to feel
weak and trembling, that had been responsible for
fourteen wakeful, lonely nights, had no connection
with lack of food. Impatiently, she brushed a hand
across her wet cheeks and forced herself to bite
into one of the sandwiches Sabelita had reluctantly
prepared and then handed over with the tight-
lipped comment,

'It is not right that a bride of two weeks should
be spending all her days alone in the wood! And as
if that in itself were not worrying enough,' she had
snapped with an anger that had hidden real
concern, 'each morning I discover that there are
two beds to be made, two rooms to be dusted, two
sets of pillows lying smooth and unused!'

Taking the coward's way out, Frances had grabbed her sandwiches and run away from questions that she, too, would have liked to have had answered, away from the husband whose glaring indifference was breaking her heart.

When her leafy hide rustled she did not look up, deciding in her misery that the cause was probably one of the sudden gusts of wind that the gypsies attributed to the devil sneezing.

'No wonder you appear to be losing weight when your lunch consists of no more than bread and tears, *amiga*!' Rom's voice accused dryly.

Like the wings of a startled bird, her lashes rose from her tear-dampened cheeks and all movement froze as instinctively she retreated behind the barrier of seclusion that was her only defence against the husband who had just addressed her as 'friend' when previously, even though for one night only, he had whispered *cami mescri*, the Romany term for lover, as he had transported her to heaven in his arms.

The cold, dead tenor of her voice sounded shocking when she forced out an excuse that was not a total lie.

'There are occasions still when I grieve over the loss of my father, especially in surroundings such as these,' she waved a shaking hand, 'where everything combines to remind me of the many conversations we shared relating to his work.'

The bleakness stamped upon Rom's features by her instantaneous withdrawal lightened a little as he slid on to the makeshift bench he had insisted upon having erected so that the spartan discomfort of the hide might be alleviated.

'What's happening at the moment?' He trained his binoculars in the direction of the eagles' nest.

'The male has just come back,' she told him, eagerly following his example, enthusiasm surging into her voice as she peered through the lenses. 'The female has come off her eggs . . . I think the male is bringing her food.'

'Yes, he is,' Rom nodded, focusing keenly.

'He's a wonderful provider,' Frances enthused, able for the first time since their wedding night to shake off the paralysing shyness imposed by the realisation that, like a new toy, she had provided a few hours of amusement and then been discarded in favour of better loved, more exciting pursuits. 'Before egg laying, the male was making as many as thirteen trips a day fetching the female food far in excess of the amount that she would normally need, but now that the eggs have been laid and she has been incubating for the last three or four days he's enjoying a well earned rest, catching only a few lizards a day to keep her going. Doesn't she look excited! And just listen to the noisy male— I'm certain he's saying, "Here you are, darling, I've brought you your lunch!"'

She could have bitten out her racing tongue when Rom lowered his binoculars and reached towards hers, moving them away to ensure that he could rely upon her complete attention.

'Motherhood, even prospective motherhood, appears to cast a potent spell over females. Fathers, on the other hand, strike me as being in the unenviable position of having no hold upon their children's affection other than the need they have of his protection.' He hesitated, appearing to consider his words carefully. 'I've heard it said that a woman forgets to be a wife once she becomes a mother, Frances. Is this true, do you suppose? Could *you* find happiness and fulfilment within a tightly knit world that neither requires nor desires the intrusion of a husband?'

She swallowed convulsively, feeling humiliation fastening a tight grip upon her throat. Yet at the same time, she experienced a small spurt of gratitude for the delicacy with which he had managed to indicate the course he wished their marriage to take. He could have been brutally frank by pointing out that she had received everything he had promised she would receive in return for a son, that he had been both angered and embarrassed by the slavish adoration she had lavished upon a bridegroom who had made love to his bride on their wedding night in the manner of a rapacious Moor. This way, he had at least allowed her to keep a little of her dignity, had given her a chance to retrieve a few shreds of pride.

'How could I help being happy were I to be the recipient of love given without reservation, a love that does not have to be fought for, and may not even be deserved,' she responded simply. 'I've prayed that I might be allowed to fulfil my side of our bargain, and if ever I should be blessed with the good fortune of giving birth to a child, the supreme happiness of knowing that for the rest of my life I shall have someone to love, someone who loves me, will be all the reward I shall need.'

Her sole aim had been to relieve Rom of an unwanted burden of responsibility, yet when he handed back her binoculars so that she might resume her vigil his features looked even grimmer than usual, his eyes masked with the closed-in look of a hooded eagle.

Made nervous by a depth of silence she could not begin to fathom, Frances began babbling an endless stream of questions to which, whenever politeness demanded, he responded with stiff, stilted answers.

'I know that the Spanish imperial eagle is classed as one of the rarest birds in the world, but what does that mean in terms of numbers?' she asked.

'We don't know. It is difficult to be exact because of the eagle's environment. Because it spends most of its time below a canopy of leaves, we don't see it all that often. However, if you wish me to hazard a guess, I'd say about a dozen birds—although some might argue that there are even less.'

Peering through her glasses at the impressive female preening her feathers, Frances commented, 'You must have formed some theory as to the cause of the birds' decline? I think they're plain silly to nest in low places where there's a very real danger of rats and other small mammals finding the nest and destroying it. One would imagine that the message would have sunk in by now and that the eagles would have begun following the example of others of their species by building their nests in more remote areas, somewhere with precipitous cliffs, for instance.'

Frowning deeply, Rom nodded agreement. 'As you say, one of the causes of decline must be that other animals find it easy to climb up to accessible

nests to steal eggs and young. But personally I
believe that their decline can be blamed mainly
upon change of habitat owing to man's wanton
destruction of the countryside. Like the gypsies,
the eagle has adopted this region as his home
because over the years it has provided safety and
food in plenty. The bird has evolved a type of
flight and style of hunting that fits his habitat, he
depends for food upon native lizards, and in turn
the lizards are dependent upon native vegetation.
As more and more trees have been cut down the
very nature of the woods has changed, normal
structure has been lost, and the consequent lack of
high density has forced the lizards to leave in
search of more congenial surroundings. As the
population of lizards has decreased, so too has the
bird population. Since we began studying the
eagles in detail there have never been more than
two or three nest sites in any one year. Last year
there was no breeding at all, so you can imagine
my relief when I was informed that one breeding
pair had been sighted.'

He frowned deeply. 'If only your father had not
died! I was so certain that he would be able to
come up with a solution, was relying heavily upon
his knowledge to help save the precious birds from
extinction. You see, Frances, from various hints
contained in his letters, I had formed the opinion
that he had a solution in mind which he did not
wish to commit to paper until he had seen for
himself the eagles' habits and habitat. But now,' he
shrugged, 'it appears inevitable that the species
must continue to decline.'

'Not necessarily.'

Even to her own ears the quiet statement seemed to bounce around the enclosed confine of the hide. She nerved herself to meet Rom's incredulous look, trembling in her anxiety to acquaint him with a solution so simple she wondered why it had taken so long to materialise.

'Some years ago a species of kestrel was similarly endangered,' she responded to his hard look of enquiry. 'It was suffering severely in the wild, so Father decided that the only way to ensure its salvation was to breed it in captivity.'

'And how did he manage to do that?' Rom rapped, obviously keen to clutch at any straw.

'First of all, he climbed up to the kestrel's nest and took the eggs.'

'*He took the eggs?*'

'Yes,' she nodded. 'It isn't as shocking as it must sound, because although he was working purely on a hunch, experience had taught him that there was every chance that the female would lay again and, as a bonus, might even decide to nest in a place of complete safety to ensure protection for her second clutch of eggs.'

'And his theory was proved correct?'

'In every respect,' she assured him, starry-eyed. 'In that same season there were twice as many kestrels, one clutch hatched in the wild, the other in captivity.'

'*Madre de Dios!*' Rom breathed, smiling down at her as if she were a messenger sent from heaven. Then just as suddenly as it had appeared his smile vanished, leaving him with a look of brooding despondency. 'What a pity your father did not have time to train someone to follow in his

footsteps—hatching out chicks and rearing them
in captivity calls for a great deal of specialised
knowledge.'

'But he did!' Frances glowed, made absurdly
happy by the thought that, should she be denied
the joy of bearing Rom's child, she would at least
be able to ensure the continuity of his beloved
eagles. 'I typed all my father's notes, kept watch
over the eggs, and helped to hand-rear the chicks
with very few problems. I'm certain I can do it
again, Rom—if you'll allow me to try!'

For the span of a few seconds he hesitated,
obviously torn between an instinct to try to ensure
the birds' survival by traditional methods and an
urge to risk an experiment that had been proved
successful—though in much more experienced
hands. But then, as if her wide appealing eyes, her
mute urging, had finally tipped the balance in her
favour, he confirmed his agreement with the
simple question,

'What equipment will you need?'

'A ladder long enough to reach the nest and
sufficient cottonwool to fill the wide-necked
thermos flask that will be needed to transport the
eggs to an incubator. I have one here!' eagerly she
swung round in search of the flask that had held
her coffee. 'This will serve nicely to keep the eggs
warm until I manage to fix up a permanent
incubator at the Palacio.'

'Fate must have prompted me to drive an estate
wagon instead of my own car,' he decided with a
grin that implied he was finding her enthusiasm
infectious. 'If its equipment is up to standard, we
ought to find an extension ladder in the back as

well as a first aid box containing sufficient
cottonwool for your needs. I'll go and check, I
shouldn't be away more than twenty minutes.'

Left to herself, Frances continued studying the
movements of the eagles, blessing, for once, their
penchant for building their huge, sprawling nests
in the lower branches of trees instead of high as a
typical eyrie. She tilted her glasses to follow the
ascent of the magnificent male bird when suddenly
it soared above the treetops and began circling
slowly upwards on immense, outstretched wings. It
was a king of birds, possessing a majestic presence
shared, she mused, with one other whose striking
snow-white markings and air of grave self-
possession stamped him with an air of authority.

If Sabelita's romantic assertions were to be
believed, it might be that one day she, too, would
be preening like the mother bird guarding her nest,
excited by the prospect of giving birth to a strong,
healthy egret who would ensure the continuity of a
family that had adopted Andalusia as its home
during the far-off days of the Moorish dynasty.

Rom's arrival put an end to her daydreams, but
some trace of her thoughts must have lingered,
making her mist-grey eyes appear dazed, wide with
apprehension.

'Are you confident of your ability to carry out
this exercise, Frances?' He hesitated with the
ladder propped on one shoulder, dark eyes delving
her expression for any hint of uncertainty. 'You do
realise, I hope, that there is an element of danger
attached to this project, that the birds could react
viciously to having their nest raided? Naturally, I
mean to protect you to the best of my ability,

nevertheless,' he trailed off, looking darkly
doubtful, 'if you have any misgivings at all, now is
the time to air them.'

Alert to the possibility that even at this late
stage he might decide to change his mind, she
continued lightly stuffing the thermos flask with
cottonwool and willed her reply to sound
businesslike and efficient.

'Birds of the wild are notoriously unpredictable.
Let's face each problem as it arises, shall we? If
you wouldn't mind propping the ladder against the
tree trunk and holding it steady?' She nodded in
the direction of the tree where the birds were
nesting as an incentive to him to get the
experiment under way. 'I'll nip up now while the
female is off the nest and the male is busy
hunting.'

No sooner had Rom adjusted the height of the
ladder and positioned it aslant with its feet dug
firmly into soft earth than she began her ascent,
nipping nimbly up each rung, using one hand as
an anchor and nursing the essential thermos flask
in the other.

She had almost reached the top, her head level
with the nest, when a bloodcurdling squawk from
the female eagle told her that she had been
spotted. She tensed, rigid, but did not look round
in case she should overbalance, then she heard
Rom quietly encouraging,

'Carry on, Frances. The female has alighted on
a branch to the left of you, behind your head. She
appears agitated, but I doubt if she will attack
before the male returns. Hurry, *cara*, get the eggs
into the flask as quickly as possible. I have a

shotgun. If necessary, I'll frighten both birds away by shooting a few blasts in the air, although I'd very much prefer not to!'

With her heart hammering, her ears deafened by the sound of a volley of screeched abuse coming from somewhere very close behind her, Frances stretched a hand above her head and began groping blindly inside the nest until her fingers closed around a delicate eggshell. Gently, her nerves tense as bowstrings, she plucked the egg out of the foul-smelling nest and transferred it to the thermos flask. Three times she repeated the action, rustling her fingers through the mound of woven sticks and caked-on mud until her mouth, eyes and ears were filled with dust, her nerves paralysed with fear of the furiously angry female that had shifted near enough to allow her to glimpse a vicious-looking beak, bloodstained bib, and sharp pointed talons. Yet from somewhere she found courage enough to remain searching until she had satisfied herself that the nest was completely empty before starting a cautious, guilt-ridden descent.

She was halfway down the ladder when the male bird reappeared, swooping in response to his mate's squawks of hysteria. With a shriek of rage that riveted Frances' feet to the rung, he began a dive bomb attack upon the ladder, forcing her to cringe in terror from the brush of powerful wings that left in its wake a slip-stream of air so strong she was almost toppled from her perch. Seconds later she screamed aloud when she was plucked from the ladder by a grip that pinched and borne through the air like some terrified victim of a winged predator.

It was not until her feet came in contact with the ground and Rom's voice shouted an order to take cover that she realised that it was he who had plucked her from the ladder and not—as her terrified senses had suggested—the huge male eagle.

'Quickly, into the hide!' Rom followed up his command with a push that sent her staggering under cover just as the swooping male bird began advancing to begin a second attack.

Rom followed her inside, and without giving her time to regain her breath, urgently demanded,

'Did you get the eggs?'

'Yes, three,' she managed to gasp in spite of a mouthful of dust and a throat dry with terror. 'They felt lukewarm when I lifted them from the nest, but I don't think the female has been sitting very tight, she's probably been keeping them cool for a while before warming them up gradually. Screw the top on the flask, would you, please,' she requested shakily. 'It's imperative that the same degree of temperature is maintained until we get the eggs into an incubator.'

'I shan't feel happy until that is done.' Quickly, he did as she had asked, before striding towards the observation space built into the wall of the hide. Sensing his concern about the upset caused to a female deprived of her eggs, and a male enraged by their encroachment upon his territory, Frances urged,

'Rom, are the birds still agitated?'

He picked up his binoculars to peer closely.

'Madre de Dios!' she heard him breathe. 'I can hardly believe it—the female is actually sitting preening!'

'I know exactly how she feels.' Lightheaded with reaction from her traumatic experience, Frances did not stop to choose her words but simply released a pent-up dam of relief and gratitude. 'Any maiden in distress would be flattered to be rescued by a gallant Sir Lancelot.'

She knew she was looking a mess, with dust-grimed cheeks, twigs sticking out of her hair, her hands and clothes filthy, yet when Rom swung round she saw a glint in his eyes that was akin to admiration. When he leant close to remove pieces of twig from her hair she quivered, her senses responding to the gentleness of his touch and to a look more tender than a kiss.

'You continue to confound me, *cara*,' he admitted gruffly. 'The last attribute a man ever expects to find in a woman is courage.'

At that moment, it seemed to Frances as if a fragile link had been forged between herself and the man she could not prevent herself from loving. She longed to keep his mood mellow, to wrap herself around, to snuggle, to luxuriate in the warmth of his approval, but the task she had undertaken demanded self-discipline and dedication as the price of success, so, in spite of a yearning to remain encapsulated with him for ever inside the leaf-cool atmosphere throbbing with unbelievable promise, she had no recourse but to prick the beautiful bubble.

'Rom,' she reminded him, grey eyes mourning the passing of a sweet, tender moment that might never return, 'we must get the eggs into an incubator within half an hour, at most.'

Ten minutes later she was sitting in a car that

was speeding them back to the Palacio, with the thermos flask containing the precious eggs cradled in her lap.

'Are you certain to find everything you'll need at the Palacio to construct a satisfactory incubator?' Rom queried, casting her a look of respect that gave her a heady sense of importance and hardened her already strong determination to make sure that the experiment reached a successful conclusion.

'Pretty certain,' she nodded happily. 'My father used to utilise items of kitchen equipment and even raided the greenhouse for soil warmers used to raise seedlings, and cloche covers which he swore were an invaluable aid to maintaining the temperature and humidity needed to hatch out the eggs. First of all, we must weigh, measure and number the eggs before placing them in the incubator, then during the following three weeks while we're waiting for the eggs to hatch I'll have to stay with them virtually twenty-four hours a day, even sleeping close by at night-time, so that I can keep checking the temperature.'

'You seem prepared to forfeit an entire month out of your lifetime to the hatching.' He sounded sharply concerned. 'Are you sure you are up to it? I will share your vigil whenever I can, of course, nevertheless it is inevitable that the heaviest burden will fall upon your shoulders. The success of this experiment means a great deal to me,' he frowned, 'but not so much that I am prepared to risk your complete exhaustion.'

'I won't let myself become exhausted,' Frances promised, revelling in the warmth of his concern.

'It's no use pretending that the next few weeks won't be hard, but the outcome will be well worth the effort involved. It's amazing,' she sighed blissfully, 'how easily weariness can be forgotten at the sight of a faint crack appearing in a shell, followed by a tiny pointed beak, then the entire emergency of a tired, naked, helpless little creature!'

Slightly, the car swerved off course as if the mind of its very competent driver had been momentarily diverted. Quickly she glanced his way, surprised by the uncharacteristic lapse of concentration, then sensed intuitively that his thoughts were dwelling upon their wedding night and that his words were somehow an indictment of herself when he expelled on a caustic breath,

'I have learnt never to underestimate the influence of the timid, whose strength lies in their weakness, who can scar a man's conscience even without claws!'

CHAPTER ELEVEN

A WINDOW enclosed by an iron *reja*, and opening right down to the floor, had been left slightly ajar to allow the night air to circulate around Frances' bedroom, and with it a noise of a fountain splashing in the garden far below. The trill of a nocturnal songbird and the endless din of crickets impinged upon her conscience as she drifted into and out of sleep, disturbing the rest she had been forced to take because during the past three weeks she had been secretly disobeying Rom's orders by hovering as closely and as constantly over the incubating eggs as a broody hen, snatching a couple of hours sleep at a time, catnapping in a chair set close to the incubator, refusing to delegate the responsibility of turning over the eggs every four hours in spite of the fact that a rota of helpers had been organised from estate workers whose conscientious application to duty Rom had sworn could be relied upon.

But with the instinct of a female who is aware whenever birth is imminent, she had sensed that tonight would be crucial, so wearily she threw back the covers, slid out of bed, and began groping in the darkness for her dressing-gown. It was a plain white cotton robe that buttoned from the neck down to a hem reaching to just above her ankles, so when she silently appeared on the threshold of the small room adjoining the kitchen that Rom had whimsically dubbed the 'maternity ward', she must have appeared to the drowsy man on duty like a ghostly apparition.

'Go to bed, José,' she smiled, wondering why his first startled reaction had been followed by a look of intense relief. 'Has there been any sign of life?' She peered through the perspex dome covering the eggs. 'Any hint of a crack in a shell?'

'Nothing, Condesa.' José rose to his feet and with a sad shake of his head prepared to take his leave. Everyone knew that the young Condesa had taken upon herself an impossible task, but she had refused to listen to reason, seemed almost to have turned a little *loca* during her bid to prove that the offspring of the Spanish imperial eagle could be treated like those of a farmyard fowl.

'Are you certain that El Conde will not mind if I leave?' Uneasily, he shuffled his feet on the stone-flagged floor. 'He was most insistent.'

'Don't worry.' Absently, already absorbed in her vigil, Frances waved him on his way. 'I shall accept entire responsibility for your absence.'

As soon as the door had closed behind him she pulled a chair close up to the table holding the incubator and sat hunched, an elbow propped on one knee, chin resting on her hand, staring hard, willing some sign of movement from eggs upon which she had lavished time, care and devotion in the hope of being able to present to her wealthy husband a gift that money could not buy. Patiently she watched, with a tender, musing smile upon her lips, while minutes ticked into hours that slipped silently by. Not once, during weeks spent watching and waiting, had the scepticism of those around

her been allowed to shake her belief that the
miracle of birth was evolving within the fragile
shells—thriving as surely and steadily as the child
that had chosen to make its tiny presence known
by inflicting upon its mother bouts of early
morning sickness.

Suddenly she was alerted out of her state of
happy euphoria by the suspicion of a crack, thin as
a pencil mark, that had appeared on the surface of
one of the mottled brown eggs. Conscious that her
competence as a midwife was about to be tested,
she removed the egg from the metal bars of the
incubator and laid it gently in a shallow bowl lined
with soft tissue. Like an echo from the past, she
recalled her father's voice, urging her to encourage
the chick out of its shell.

*'When the chicks are hatching, the mother bird,
the incubating female, talks to the chicks as they are
emerging, reassuring them by giving chirping
vocalisations. Try to imitate her baby talk.'*

After a nervous gulp, Frances leant close to the
egg and attempted the mother-bird's vocal aid to
delivery.

'Ch.i.r.r.r.p! Ch.i.r.r.r.p! *Push!* Ch.i.r.r.r.p! Come
on! *Heave!'* she pleaded. 'Come on, my precious,
h.e.a.v.e . . .!'

At that precise moment, just as the tip of a tiny
beak pierced a hole in the shell, it seemed entirely
appropriate that Rom should materialise as if
from nowhere, standing close enough for her to
hear his sharply indrawn breath, and to share her
joy at the sight of the eggshell cracking gradually,
piece by piece, then finally falling away to reveal a
skinny, damp, weary, yet healthy-looking egret.

The other two chicks followed its example by emerging in quick succession, leaving them no time to voice their joy and wonder until all three chicks were nestling sweetly inside a box lined with straw constructed and contoured as nearly as possible along the lines of the nest from which the eggs had been removed.

Dawn had broken, and sounds made by servants moving around the interior of the Palacio could be heard, when Frances clasped her hands as if offering a prayer of thanksgiving and turned to Rom with an ecstatic sigh.

'Triplets! A new set of triplets for the Aquila family!'

'Thanks entirely to you, *chica madre*,' Rom breathed, keeping his glance locked with hers as slowly as he drew her towards him. His dark head, tousled by raking fingers, was lowering to place a kiss of gratitude upon her quivering mouth when the door was flung open by José, who had obviously decided to return to relieve Frances of her vigil.

'*Que mona! Muy bonita!*' His cry of delight at the sight of the chicks fetched the rest of the servants running and seconds later the room was filled with an uproar of excitedly babbling people.

'Outside, everyone! Outside!' Looking slightly exasperated, Rom shooed the servants into the kitchen, then, relenting at the sight of their downcast faces, he ordered with a grin, 'Fetch champagne! We must all drink to the health of the new arrivals!'

Anxious to check up on the welfare of the chicks, Frances slipped unnoticed inside the room filled with the sound of hungry chirping and discovered José busily preparing their first feed.

'If you will allow me, Condesa,' he requested almost apologetically, 'I should like to be put in sole charge of the little egrets. Once begun, a task becomes easy. All the important work has been done by you, but the unpleasant task of keeping them supplied with a constant stream of worms, insects and grubs is unsuitable for pale soft hands and can be safely left to me.'

'As it shall be, José.' A protest died on Frances' lips when Rom strode inside carrying a glass of champagne. 'Drink this up,' he commanded sternly. 'As soon as you have finished it you must return to your room to catch up on your rest, and this time,' he breathed the promise under his breath, 'I shall make certain that you stay there.'

Impelled by his black crystal look, she forced herself to drink the raw gold liquid that burst bubbles under her nose and fermented the sweet taste of happiness to a pitch of sparkling exhilaration that rushed straight to her head, making her feel giddy. The sensation of floating on a cloud intensified when Rom scooped her into his arms to carry her out of the kitchen and up the sweeping staircase to her room.

She strove hard to disperse the weariness that was threatening to cut short the most glorious period of fulfilment she had ever known, and to deny her the pleasure of seeing Rom as she had seen him only once previously—on the night that passion inherited from the combination of gypsy and Moorish blood had been given rein, allowed to outstrip the cool hauteur of the Spanish grandee, the indifference of a lofty Lord of the Land.

It was nice to feel cossetted, she decided, when he deposited her gently upon her bed, nice to feel petted and pampered, to know that she had pleased him sufficiently to be rewarded with the exquisite pleasure of feeling his teeth tenderly nibbling her ear, of experiencing once again the utter bliss of being cradled in arms that seemed determined never to let her go. Exerting great effort of will, she forced heavy lashes to lift over wine-drugged eyes. Tiredness was enveloping her like a cloak, a cloak which for weeks she had determinedly pushed aside, preventing herself through sheer strength of will from succumbing to its sleep-inducing warmth.

'Your eyes remind me of the grey fathomless depths of mountain tarns, *cami mescri*, the *ojos del mar* which shepherds believe show signs of disturbance whenever a storm threatens even from many miles away.'

Rom's voice sounded strangely disembodied, yet tight with leashed emotion.

'Legend has endowed one of these tarns with special mystery. In its depths, so it is said, is a palace built by a Moorish king, in which a beautiful slave girl grieves for the master who abandoned her. This grief leads her to draw down into the depths any man who dares to wander near, appearing to them in the form of a timid white bird that tempts them to the edge of calm grey waters then pulls them below to drown in the ecstasy of her arms. I feel like a victim of that timid white bird, *querida*,' his whispered words seemed to be gradually fading, 'charmed by the wiles of a grey-eyed temptress . . .'

'Rom,' she murmured, feeling herself drifting into a chasm of darkness yet worried by a reminder that there was something very important that she had forgotten to tell him.

'Yes, *querida* . . .?'

She smothered a yawn, the pounding of his heart against her cheek imposing the hypnotic effect of a steadily beating drum.

'. . . please remember to tell José that when he feeds the chicks he must cut up the worms very small.'

She awoke after almost eight hours of sleep feeling fretful. Drowsily, she lay looking around the room kept cool and dim by shutters closed against the heat of the noonday sun, her brow puckering into lines of worry as she tried to recall the misty interlude she had shared with Rom just before sleep had claimed her. But her subconscious refused to release any clue as to why she should be feeling so cheated, why an inner voice should be insisting that for a few precious seconds supreme happiness had beckoned and then sorrowfully passed her by.

A light tap upon the door preceded Sabelita's entry into the room carrying a tray laden with her mistress's favourite breakfast—lightly boiled egg, toast, and a tall pot spouting the rich, aromatic smell of freshly percolated coffee.

'Ah, so you are awake at last!' Sabelita beamed, advancing towards the bed. 'It is almost lunchtime, but I thought you might prefer to eat in your room?'

Frances nodded agreement and eagerly eased herself upright, propping her shoulders against a bank of pillows. But immediately she caught sight of the food-laden tray a wave of nausea struck, draining colour from her cheeks, rendering grey eyes dark with apprehension.

'Oh!' Her sharp cry of distress brought Sabelita to an enquiring halt, then when Frances struggled out of bed clasping a hand over her mouth and rushed towards the bathroom comprehension dawned and a great smile of happiness transformed the old gypsy's features.

She had disposed of the tray and was hurrying to render assistance when Frances reappeared, clutching the doorframe for support, looking spent and ashen.

'Don't worry, *chica*,' the old woman scolded happily. 'The sickness will soon pass and *then* . . .!' she heaved an ecstatic sigh, '. . . oh, the joy I shall feel when I hold the new baby in my arms! The rejoicing that will erupt the moment my tribe is told the news! Such an outcome was inevitable, of course,' she beamed, 'yet never before have I known the *albahaca* magic to work so swiftly.'

'No, Sabelita!' In spite of the weakness of her voice Frances managed to project a note of authority. 'You must tell no one—not yet.'

'But El Conde will insist upon spreading the news!'

'Not even he must know,' Frances shocked the old servant, who considered that every husband had a right to be told immediately his wife became aware that she was expecting his child—and *especially* El Conde!

Frances' heart sank when Sabelita's mouth tightened mutinously. She braced to combat arguments she knew were justified, knowing that she could supply no satisfactory explanation for a decision that even she found puzzling. The reason Rom had asked her to become his wife had been made cruelly explicit. He needed an heir, but had no wish to become emotionally involved with the mother of his child. He was a man who could love only one woman in his lifetime—a man who, because he had once handed his heart into the keeping of a girl who had proved fickle, had decided for the rest of his life to remain heartless . . .

To her utter dismay she felt tears spurting into her eyes. Rapidly she blinked, then turned aside hoping to hide her misery, but realised when she heard a hissed-in breath that the wise old woman had seen and interpreted her tears correctly.

'You think that your man does not want you, that he is in love with another,' she claimed softly. 'That must not be. Trust me, child. As the young Isabella once proved, there are spells potent enough to draw down the moon; love philtres with the magic to make a man besotted.'

Frances' bowed head jerked erect. 'No, Sabelita! You must not attempt to mix any of your weird concoctions into El Conde's drinks—I absolutely forbid it.'

'Very well, Bori Rani.' Somehow, Sabelita's deferential response did not ring true, her expression was too bland, her eyes bright with wicked cunning, especially when she reminded,

'Have you forgotten that today is the day you

have agreed to accompany Señorita Peralta and her guests to the *corrida* that is staged annually by their local villagers? The bullfight afternoon is regarded as a very special occasion; everyone dresses up. Usually, six bulls are killed, every one of them hand-picked from the herd belonging to the Marqués de Quesada, Señorita Peralta's father. Each bull is killed according to the time-honoured ritual known as the *lidia*. Each *lidia* takes about twenty minutes and three *matadors* kill two bulls each during their own separate *lidias*. First, three bulls are killed, then after a short intermission, the *matadors* dispose of the remaining three.'

If her aim had been to take Frances' mind off their previous discussion she could not have chosen a subject more likely to succeed. With a groan of disgust, Frances swung round and disappeared into the bathroom, slamming the door behind her.

But little more than an hour later, after a refreshing shower and a leisurely period of relaxation, the absence of nausea helped to revive her spirits, even to the extent of making her wish that she had something colourful and exotic to wear. As yet, the proud Conde did not appear to have noticed the glaring discrepancies in his wife's wardrobe. Frances sighed, reaching for the plain white dress that had seen so much service, but which would have to be worn yet again.

She was standing in front of a mirror, wearing the thin silk slip that doubled as a lining for her dress, critically eyeing a neckline and shoulders gleaming pale as magnolia blossoms that hid behind large glossy leaves from harsh rays of sunlight, when a knock upon the door jerked from her lips the startled response,

  'Adelante!'

Expecting to see Sabelita or one of the young maids, she swung round, then stared, the smile of greeting freezing on her lips.

'Sabelita has hunted out these dresses.' Rom strode past to dump an armful of brilliant satins and shimmering silks upon her bed. 'I owe you an apology, *cara*, it should not have been necessary for a servant to have to point out to me my wife's needs. Soon,' he promised, 'we will fly to Cordova—or better still, Seville, which is the city Maria appears to favour whenever she feels an urge to go shopping. I must admit that Sabelita's pointed references to your lack of suitable clothes surprised me.' He frowned down at her, apparently unaware of her shivering embarrassment. 'You have never seemed to be particularly concerned about your appearance.'

Perhaps it was his betrayal of a close knowledge of Maria's movements that caused her hackles to rise, or maybe what some might have termed her 'delicate condition' was responsible for an unmistakable note of petulance that caused his black winged eyebrows to soar.

'Even the best-dressed show falls flat without an interested audience,' she snapped. 'However, as you appear to move in the sort of circles that judge a woman's worth by the price tag on her dress, I suppose I'd better choose something to wear from these ancient cast-offs!'

She knew it was wrong of her to cast a look of disparagement at the costly, beautifully hand-sewn dresses that had been slid out of the fine cambric covers into which they had been stitched before being stored in chests redolent of lavender and sandalwood.

'All Spanish girls wear the full, flounced gowns of old Spain for the *feria*,' Rom quietly shamed her by saying. 'Even the men are not above entering into the spirit of things by wearing Cordoba hats, tight jackets and leather *chaparajos* if they intend riding on horseback.'

He sounded determined to be kind, to curb the whip-sharp sting of impatience that never failed to cast a shadow across the face of his young bride.

'What's wrong, Frances?' he urged softly, then checked his movement towards her, obviously puzzled by her shrinking retreat, slightly bitter mouth, and eyes clouded dark with pain. 'If you are not feeling up to it, we could cancel our visit to the ranch.'

'And what would Maria say to that?' Displaying the temperament of a Spanish *condesa*, she flounced across to the window and stood with her back turned, willing her trembling to cease, wondering why, instead of revelling in his unusual show of tenderness, she should feel compelled to be contrary.

Angrily he confirmed her suspicion that it had been foolish of her to remind him of the girl whose rejection had scarred him to such an extent that he had married a nobody just to get even.

'What man would be idiot enough to claim insight into the workings of the devious female mind? Certainly not I,' he glowered, savagely abandoning all pretence of patience. 'Woman is like your shadow. Follow her and she flies. Fly from her and she follows!'

She turned on him with sparkling eyes, fiercely glad to have aroused any emotion stronger than the gratitude which she now knew could never be enough.

'Maria and yourself are so ideally suited,' she flared, 'I can't understand why you decided to marry *me*!'

'Perhaps I was influenced by the ancient gypsy adage that advises: *"In buying horses and in taking a wife, shut your eyes and trust in God",*' he responded wrathfully. 'Sadly, my trust appears to have been misplaced!'

Her wince of pain did nothing to improve his temper. Grim-faced, he strode across to a chair, sat down, and flicked his fingers in the direction of the dresses piled upon the bed.

'Time is running short. Make a choice, if you please. I'll wait here to deliver my verdict.'

'There's no need,' she blushed miserably. 'With Sabelita's help I'm sure to find something suitable.'

'As Sabelita's taste runs to vulgar colour schemes, and your own is an unknown entity, I wish to approve your appearance before presenting you to friends eager to meet my new bride. Wear anything but white—the colour of innocence is no longer appropriate,' he reminded her cruelly. 'Try pink, to match the shamed colour that is seldom absent from your cheeks. Or blue, because it does something extraordinary to your eyes. As you may have noticed while studying portraits of previous *Condesas* hung around the Palacio walls, my lusty ancestors showed a definite preference for wives who were physically well endowed—passionate, flirtatious-looking coquettes who knew how to excite their husbands' interest with a daring show of cleavage. You might do well to follow the example of your predecessors, Frances,' he mocked her fiery cheeks and downcast lashes. 'I doubt if any one of them was ever indifferent to her husband's advances, ever allowed her thoughts to linger in the kitchen when her services were required in the bedroom.'

Frances turned aside, deciding to ignore the hardbitten challenge that she did not understand but which she sensed was meant to be hurtful. With a heavy heart and only desultory interest, she began rifling through dresses that had been worn long ago by women in love eager to give pleasure to men who loved them.

Satin, grey and soothing as a marble-floored mosque dappled with colours tossed by sunshine through a stained glass window. Silk, shimmering and scented as lamps holding aromatic oils. Lace, black and scrolled as grilles spread around balconies and in front of windows secreted within courtyards where blossoms splashed painfully vivid against stark white walls.

The fragrance of orange blossom seemed to drift beneath her nostrils when she lifted from the pile a puff-sleeved, full-skirted dress of unsophisticated design, printed with sprigs of green, and rosemary petals massed into misty-blue posies strewn against a crisp white cotton background.

'I like this one!'

She swung round holding the dress in front of

her, ready to defend her choice, knowing that its simple, unpretentious lines exactly suited her personality.

'Somehow, I suspected that you might.'

To her relief, Rom no longer sounded angry, just mildly resigned.

'Very well,' he nodded, rising from his chair, 'put it on while I go and change. But be quick, enough time has been wasted. I shall expect you to be ready when I return in about ten minutes' time.'

He had opened the door and was about to step across the threshold when Sabelita appeared outside in the passageway carrying a tray containing glasses and a tall frosted jug of *limonada*.

'Before you leave, you must try some of this, Rom Boro,' she insisted firmly. 'I've made it specially for you!'

Hastily, she set the tray down upon a nearby table and poured out a small glassful. He hesitated, then obviously deciding that it would be quicker to drink than to argue, he accepted the drink with a shrug.

He had raised the glass almost to his lips when Frances happened to glance Sabelita's way and realised with a sudden sense of shock that the obstinate old gypsy was gloating over the ease with which she had managed to persuade Rom to accept the drink—a drink that probably contained herb and plant juices that might inflict irreparable harm, might be poisonous, might even drive a man insane!

'*No*, Rom—*don't*!'

Surprised by her anguished cry, he hesitated,

glancing from her shocked face to Sabelita's
uneasy expression. Then to her horror she saw an
inscrutable smile appear on his lips before he
tossed back his head and deliberately drained the
glass dry.

CHAPTER TWELVE

Rom piloted the helicopter to the ranch of the Marqués de Quesada and immediately the craft touched down on a landing pad situated inside the cattle baron's estate they saw a car approaching swiftly from the direction of an adjacent hacienda. The servant who alighted had obviously been instructed to tender profuse apologies.

'Many pardons, Señor Conde—Señora Condesa—for the absence of your host. As the Marqués was eager to extend a personal welcome, he delayed his departure for as long as good manners permitted. However, the *corrida* cannot begin before his arrival, so he felt bound to leave for the bullring where his presence was required for the official opening. The crowd was growing impatient,' he explained to Frances. 'To the Andalusian, the *corrida* is not regarded merely as entertainment but is a fever in the blood. All the best *matadors* come from Andalusia,' he boasted proudly. 'A knowledgeable spectator can, at a glance, tell an Andaluz from any other bullfighter by his sensuous grace, his proud demeanour, his grave unflinching way of staring death in the face!'

As if sensing her shudder of repugnance, Rom stemmed the servant's eulogy with the curt request,

'There is no need to apologise, the fault is ours for arriving late. If you would be good enough to drive us,' he stared pointedly towards the car, 'the Condesa and I would like to join our host without further delay.'

As they were being driven at breakneck speed past the deserted *hacienda* and along roads ribboning the Marqués's estate, Rom mused ruefully,

'In a way, it is a pity that your first impression of the bullfight will lack all the splendour and pageant attached to the major stadiums where, high up in the stands opposite the bullfighters' entrance, the President of the Corrida sits flanked by officials and thousands of excited fans, signalling the beginning or the end of each act by waving a white handkerchief to watching trumpeters who then blast out his interpreted signals.'

'Each act?' Frances queried, looking apprehensive as a child in her simple flower-sprigged dress. 'You speak as if we were about to attend an opera!'

The smouldering intensity of his look raced a sweep of wild colour to her cheeks. From the moment he had spun on his heel to watch her rushing like a flustered maidservant into the presence of her master waiting impatiently in the hall, he had reverted once more to the attitude she found confusing—a mood of leashed-in tenderness which, had he been anyone other than the imperious Lord of the Land, might have been blamed upon uncertainty, upon the unwillingness of a clumsy-footed male to trespass upon ground more fragile than eggshells.

Quickly, she turned her head aside in case her eyes should betray her secret, in case he should guess that simply because his blood had mingled with hers, because for one magical night he had made her feel that she was the only other person in the world, had held her spellbound, had made her feel powerfully, mysteriously, sensuously possessed; and because she could feel his child's heartbeat, feeble as a pulse, beating in time with her own, that she resented his gratitude and was suffering all the symptoms of a jealous, possessive *wife*!

'The comparison is very apt.' In spite of her shrinking withdrawal his voice remained determinedly goodhumoured. 'The killing of a bull is a drama in three acts. The first act is the "trial" when the *picadors* on horseback demonstrate the mettle of the bull to the watching crowd. The second act, the "sentencing" is when the *banderillos'* darts intensify the bull's rage and then sober him up, changing from a beast who wants to kill everything in sight to one who becomes crafty as he realises that he is about to begin fighting for his life. The last act is the kill, during which the *matador* uses his cape to display his domination of the bull, making him do whatever he wants, whenever he wants, so that he charges at exactly the right moment to afford spectators the sight of a perfect kill.'

Feeling a heaving in the pit of her stomach, Frances concentrated hard upon dispersing a squeamish urge to beg to be allowed to miss the gory spectacle, but even as a plea was trembling on her lips a loud roar of approval attracted her attention ahead towards what appeared to be an enclosure with bodies craning over every square inch of its wooden walls. At the farthest end its symmetry was broken by a raised dais that had a gaily striped awning protecting the heads of its seated occupants from glaring sunrays. As she stepped from the car she glimpsed a hot yellow circle of sand and a gate in the wooden wall opening inward. Suddenly the crowd became hushed, staring expectantly towards the black void into which no sunlight was penetrating.

'Rom! At last, *caro*, you have arrived!'

Maria, wearing a black lace mantilla and with a carnation the colour of her pouting, crimson lips tucked behind one ear, stepped down from the dais to greet them, groomed to the last eyelash, a riveting spectacle of old-world aristocratic finery.

Flicking Frances a look that made her feel a dowdy, travel-stained, creased and crumpled mess of querulous womanhood, Maria ushered them towards two seats that had been left vacant, attempting a swift introduction to the rest of her guests above the roar of a crowd noisily animated by the sight of a bull hurtling through the void into the sun-scorched arena.

The clatter of his entry died as his hoofs bit the sand. The bewildered animal paused, dazzled by his sudden emergence from darkness, then spotting the flicker of a red cape over the wooden wall he trotted a few steps, lowered his haunches and began digging his hoofs deeper into the sand. Vaguely, Frances registered the touch of Rom's hand upon her arm while she stared with a mixture of horror and fascination at the magnificent black animal that had begun running with his head slightly lowered, iron-hard muscles rippling as he dipped his horns to ram the infuriating cape. But at the crucial moment the cape was whipped back over the wooden fence and the bull, deprived of any sight of movement, veered away snorting angrily, his stride lengthening as he sought a fresh source of aggravation.

'He is a magnificent beast, is he not, Condesa!'

Surprise distracted Frances's gaze away from the bullring in search of the owner of the feminine voice whose meaningful stresses had left her in no doubt that the subject of interest was not the tormented animal pawing the sand below. Her pulses leapt with panic when her dazed eyes met Maria's glittering stare. Unknown to herself, she and Rom had changed places, probably to make it easier for him to exchange conversation with the frail, elderly gentleman seated on his left whom she had heard introduced as the Marqués de Quesada. 'Like myself,' Maria continued to confirm her theory, 'Rom is the product of a hard, harsh land, of a people who have often felt the brush of disaster but who would fight to the death rather than suffer the humiliation of seeing their pride dragged in the dust!'

Making no attempt to prevaricate, Frances bravely picked up the gauntlet Maria had flung.

'I'm sorry if you have been made to feel humiliated, *señorita*.' In spite of her low, shaken response she somehow managed to retain an air of quiet dignity. 'It is a pity, as you appear to regard Rom as your personal property, that you didn't marry him at the time when he was so much in love with you.'

'Why do you speak in the past tense?' Maria's

mocking self-assurance could not be doubted. In spite of brilliant sunshine, the atmosphere of festive excitement, depression descended upon Frances like a cloud. She did not have the weapons to fight this girl dressed like a beautiful Spanish queen, one buoyed by the knowledge that in the hearts of all her subjects—and of one especially—she reigned supreme.

When a concerted yell of encouragement drew her attention back to the bullring she saw men on horseback manoeuvring the tormented bull inside a white circle painted inside the ring, apparently inciting the beast to attack. As she watched, the bull charged as if intent upon digging his horns into the quilted padding protecting one of the horses. Swiftly, the rider raised his arm. She saw a flash of steel as the *picador* plunged his lance towards the bull's hump, then a sickening spurt of blood when the wounded beast shied off, suffering pain, surprise, and fear.

At that precise moment, the bullring, the performers, and the entire crowd began swimming before her eyes. She must have gasped aloud, for beneath the cover of frantic applause Maria's voice called,

'What's wrong? Are you feeling faint?'

Dumbly, Frances nodded, exerting every ounce of willpower to fight wave after wave of nausea.

'Don't dare to faint here!' Maria's command was totally devoid of compassion. 'Rom would never forgive such a loss of dignity. Pull yourself together and try to appear composed while I make some excuse to the others for our temporary absence.'

Frances had no idea what pretty lie Maria told,

but Rom's response, directed as if from a long way away, sounded amused, even slightly indulgent.

'Do whatever you wish, *chica madre*, you deserve a little pampering.'

Maria's reaction to the fond address, 'little mother', earned because of her success with the egrets, was a long indrawn hiss.

The events of the following few minutes passed in a blur. Somehow, with Maria's assistance, Frances managed to walk without staggering, without betraying any of the panic she felt when the ground appeared to begin rising and falling away beneath her feet. Normality returned only when she was seated in Maria's car, feeling a breeze teasing her hair and cooling her cheeks while she was being driven at maniacal speed along roads which she assumed led back to the *hacienda*.

Even when Maria stamped hard upon the brake, jolting the car to a screeching standstill miles from nowhere, Frances felt no inkling of danger, merely curiosity as to why the car should have been stopped on a deserted stretch of road flanked by endless miles of grazing land, its flatness unbroken except where tall wooden rails had been erected to form a huge, corral-type enclosure.

'Get out!' Goaded by the bewilderment evident in mist-blue eyes, Maria started towards her looking as berserk as the maddened bull whose eyes had been rolling with the lust to kill. 'Rom loves *me*!'

Frances felt the dig of sharp fingernails as she was pulled out of the car, then a thump between her shoulderblades that sent her staggering against the barred gate. *'And I love him far too much to allow any other woman to bear his child!'*

Terrified out of her wits by Maria's insane glare, Frances pressed her back against the gate and felt it give way behind her. With a laugh of pure evil, Maria darted forward to push her hard inside the enclosure before slamming the gate shut and turning a key in an iron padlock.

'Trespassers really should take more care!' Frances heard her shout gleefully as she ran back towards the car. 'If you look to your right, Condesa,' she yelled above the noise of the revving engine, 'you will see a notice that warns: *"Beware of the bull"*!'

It could not possibly be true, Frances assured herself, pressing her shaking body hard against the gate towering a foot above her head where it met the level of a fence built high enough to protect the unwary from beasts averaging a thousand pounds in weight, that could outrun a horse over short distances, that were strong enough to lift a horse and rider on their horns and toss them far enough back to fall clear of their tails. She was experiencing a nightmare from which she was sure to waken soon, a nightmare—she jerked stiff and cold with fear—*that included a black speck in the far distance that was moving menacingly towards her!*

Maria must have gone mad! The thought registered at the same instant that the noise of a car engine impinged upon her subconscious. Maria had relented, she was coming back!

Held fast in the paralysing grip of terror, Frances stood as if frozen, staring at the speck looming nearer and nearer until a body began taking shape before her frightened eyes.

The increasing proximity of a huge black body,

slobbering foam-flecked mouth, and eyes glaring madly beneath a wicked crown of horns gave her the impetus to scream, a piercing cry of terror that was answered by the squeal of brakes and Rom's frantic voice shouting an order.

'Frances, don't move! Stay very, very still!'

Gratefully, she obeyed his command by sliding slowly, helplessly, into a dead faint.

The white and gold comfort of her surroundings struck her as familiar when eventually she struggled to raise heavy eyelids over eyes still dazed with half-remembered fear. Then when realisation dawned she sighed her pleasure at having been returned home, of being surrounded by things that were safe, familiar, and well loved.

The noise, soft though it was, must have reached as far as the shuttered window where a man was standing with his back turned, head bowed as if deep in thought. When he swung on his heel she saw that it was Rom, looking somehow different— strained, haggard, deathly pale beneath his tan.

'How are you feeling now, *querida*?' His voice, too, sounded different and his movements, though swift, lacked their usual spring of vitality when he strode across to the bed.

'Fine . . .' she quavered, moved almost to tears by his expression of deep concern. 'What happened?' She frowned, attempting to recall some horror that her memory seemed reluctant to resurrect. 'Oh, now I remember!' She caught an agonised breath. 'I began feeling unwell . . . Maria offered to drive me to her home . . .' Then terror flooded back, swirling horrified disbelief into wide grey eyes. 'Rom,' she levered herself upright, *'Maria tried to kill me!'*

Gently he pressed her back against the pillows. 'Try not to judge her too harshly, *chica,*' he pleaded, deeply serious.

Her heart sank like a stone. Was he so much in love with Maria that he was about to try to excuse her dreadful behaviour? She closed her eyes to hide tears of despair and lay motionless while he quietly explained,

'Maria's emotional instability made itself known during her early teens. Naturally, as our families had always been close, I helped in every way I could to ensure that her condition was kept secret from an inquisitive world. Doctors repeatedly assured her father that there was no danger of her ever becoming violent. All that was necessary, they maintained, was that at the onset of the black moods that were symptomatic of her illness she should be confined to her room where someone could be with her every single moment. Then, when she was about eighteen,' he hesitated, then continued firmly, 'she began imagining that she was in love with me . . .'

Something deep inside Frances seemed to stir, then settled back to normal with a sigh of relief.

'Her father asked my permission—which was readily given—to act out the part of an aristocratic *hidalgo* who considered no man good enough for his only child, so that whenever she boasted to anyone that I had proposed marriage he could immediately voice a fierce objection which, as well as providing listeners with an impression that the marriage would never take place, also appeared to appease the guilt she must have suffered whenever she voiced the lie.'

Frances raised her lashes just in time to see agony reflected in eyes sober as the day of judgment, ridden dark with self-condemnation.

'Maria will never be allowed such freedom again! I cannot imagine what caused her sanity to snap when it did, but I promise you, Frances,' he stressed with a steel thread of determination running through his words, 'that never in future will she be in a position to pose any kind of threat to your safety.'

Chica madre! She felt an impulse to tell him that it had been the implication Maria had read in those two small words that had pushed her over the brink of sanity. Little mother! She chanced a sideways glance, wondering if this was the right moment to tell him that she was carrying his child, then forgot everything at the sight of his tortured expression.

'I can't remember anything about my rescue,' she admitted huskily, 'but I'm certain that you must have saved my life at the risk of your own. Thank you, Rom,' she smiled shyly, 'I'm very grateful.'

She was startled by his look of anger, by a grip that tightened as if he were resisting a temptation to shake her.

'Does a man deserve gratitude for saving his own sanity?' he grated savagely. 'My motive was purely selfish, all I wanted was to ensure that I would continued to be soothed by the calmness of your presence, delighted by an occasional glimpse of deliciously feminine hips wiggling inside masculine denim, won over by the arguments of an uncynical mind, shamed by the generosity of a heart that interprets loving as giving! I don't know exactly when your gentle grey-eyed spirit took possession of my heart, *cami mescri*,' he groaned suddenly, 'all I know is that, if a presentiment of disaster had not urged me to follow closely behind Maria's car, if I had not arrived just in time to distract the attention of the beast that was bracing itself to charge, I would have wanted to throw my own useless body on its lethal horns! I love you, my life, my adorable *chica madre*!'

He scooped her from the pillows to enclose her within the urgent cradle of his arms. '*Luz de mi vida*, promise me that you will stay, give me just one more chance to prove myself deserving of the devotion that you wore on our wedding day like a halo for all to see!'

Very much later, when she had been allowed to descend slowly from a floating cloud of ecstasy to nestle closely into the comfort and security of his arms, Frances dared to stroke tender fingers across a silver wing of hair and scold lovingly,

'I was worried in case you should be taken ill. Do you realise that the *limonada* Sabelita persuaded you to drink probably contained some of the weird substances she gathers to make up her so-called love philtres?'

She felt him stir, heard a growl of laughter deep inside his throat.

'So what if the drink *was* a love potion?' he teased, gazing down at her sweetly flushed face with the hunger of a passion starved gypsy. 'Sabelita will hear no complaint from me, *querida*, because so far as I am concerned, it worked perfectly!'

A WORD ABOUT THE AUTHOR

Margaret Rome's first Harlequin was published in 1969. Appropriately, it was entitled *A Chance to Win* (Harlequin Romance #1307).

But her chance was a while in coming. In her teens Margaret dealt with a long-term bout of rheumatic fever; then followed a series of manual jobs that "just could not satisfy my active mind," and finally marriage and the birth of a son. But at last, when Margaret did get down to the business of writing—beginning by doodling with pen and paper—she discovered that a sentence formed, a second one followed, and before long, paragraphs had developed into a chapter. "I had begun the first of many journeys," she says.

Today Margaret and her husband make their home in Northern England. For recreation they enjoy an occasional night out dancing, and on weekends they drive into the beautiful Lake District and embark on long, invigorating walks.

HARLEQUIN
REMIERE AUTHOR EDITIONS

top Harlequin authors—6 of their best books!

- **JANET DAILEY** Giant of Mesabi
- **CHARLOTTE LAMB** Dark Master
- **ROBERTA LEIGH** Heart of the Lion
- **ANNE MATHER** Legacy of the Past
- **ANNE WEALE** Stowaway
- **VIOLET WINSPEAR** The Burning Sands

Harlequin is proud to offer these 6 exciting romance novels by of our most popular authors. In brand-new beautifully esigned covers, each Harlequin Premiere Author Edition a bestselling love story—a contemporary, compelling and assionate read to remember!

vailable in September wherever paperback books are sold, *or* through arlequin Reader Service. Simply complete and mail the coupon below.